A Day to Forget

Bobo Blankson, MD
Copyright © 2018 Kwabena Blankson
All rights reserved.
ISBN-13: 978-1517451813

DEDICATION

To   Amy,   for   always   believing   in   me.

Chapter 1

5:35 A.M.

My name is Benjamin Brew. It's 5:35 in the morning, and today's my eighteenth birthday.

I roll out of bed because my bladder is screaming at me. This is not one of those "hold it for twenty-five more minutes until my alarm goes off" moments. No, this is PEECON4, and I have not been in PEECON5 since Jimmy Landry's sleepover in fourth grade, after which I swore to never wet myself again, in public or private.

I sigh because once I'm up, I'm probably not gonna fall back asleep though I'll try my darnedest. My legs clumsily carry me into the bathroom, and I'm grateful the nightlight beside the sink is providing that soft off-white glow that's just enough to guide me without sending my brain an urgent signal to wake up. I've got a killer headache.

The toilet seat is down. That's unusual. But I'm trying not to overthink right now, because I'm singularly focused on stealing twenty-four more minutes of precious sleep before I have to get up for school. I lift the seat and do my business.

I don't flush, a habit I developed over the years when I didn't want my parents to know I'd been wide awake under the covers fighting for freedom with Flint, Lady Jaye, and Cobra Commander, or reading the latest Frank and Joe Hardy *Casefiles*.

I walk back to my bed and crawl under the sheets. They're still warm. I close my eyes, flop onto my belly and smile, snuggling into my down pillow. It smells like . . . like perfume. But I'm not overthinking, I'm trying to fall back asleep for twenty-two more minutes. And I need this buzzing headache to go away.

I roll onto my left, away from the red glare of my alarm clock. The smell of perfume grows stronger. I fluff the sheets as I stretch out my arms. When my right hand lands, it doesn't sink into my quilted comforter.

It lands on . . . on something warm. I suppress my startle because my non-overthinking brain tells me it's just Bella, our Maltese poodle. But whatever is under my hand is not furry. It's soft. My fingers continue to explore. *Is that . . . is that a nipple?!*

The body underneath my frigid right hand predictably stirs, my ears catching a few nonsensical words followed by a plaintive moan. *I'm touching booby, holy shiitake!* I'm not overthinking anymore, I'm panicking. If I'm in bed with Jessica, and she's naked, and my parents find out she's here, my senior year may end prematurely.

In my panic, I notice other parts of me have become excited. *Señor Pedro, this is really bad timing.* I'm trying to figure out how I'm going to sneak Jess out of my room and out of the house (my second-floor window is

NOT an option), when all of a sudden, I hear my bedroom door creak open. I roll onto my back, eyes glued shut, breath held. My heart stops.

I'm a dead man.

Señor Pedro now acknowledges the gravity of the situation and begins a slow, protracted bow as I wait for the lights to turn on, the charade to be over, the ten-minute lecture, the public shaming, my summer-long grounding.

Instead, I hear the pitter-patter of little feet.

And then something is crawling into the bed with me, now on top of me. A curly head lies on my chest.

"Daddy, can I sleep with you?"

Something is terribly wrong.

Chapter 2

5:37 A.M.

I'm wide awake and intentionally overthinking and completely confused, my throbbing headache only getting worse. I know I'm not dreaming. There really is a little girl on top of me right now. It's taking a concerted effort to take a full breath, as I'm having to use the accessory muscles of my chest to lift her dense body AND breathe deeply. And I desperately need air because my head is swimming.

I'm a smart guy. Though my brother wouldn't use the word "guy." When he tells me I'm smart "in a Bart-Simpsony way," I suspect he's not paying me a compliment. But I'm smart enough to put two and two together. If there's a kid on my chest calling me Daddy, the naked woman beside me must be my ... *cringe* ... my baby mama.

I feel like I'm probably not going to fall back asleep at this point. I'm anticipating ... um ... a few complications today. My eighteenth birthday. Which was supposed to be an uncomplicated day. As usual, Dad's minivan would embarrassingly drop me off at the front door of Altomonte High. Third period, I would use my student pass to catch an early lunch with Jessica to celebrate my birthday *and* six months of drama-free dating. Truly an achievement for any high school couple, believe me. My parents had planned a little

4

party in the evening for me, a few friends and nearby relatives. But all of this was now an afterthought. Priority number one? Figure out what the heck is going on. I certainly don't remember getting Jessica pregnant, attending a delivery, naming a child, and being allowed to live safely, unneutered, in my parents' house. I quickly check for vasectomy scars, though I'm not really sure exactly what my fingers are looking for. Hmmm . . . both boys are present and accounted for—I think that's a good sign?

I turn my head to the right. 5:57. My eyes are finally adjusting to the darkness. I look around the room to get my bearings.

This is not my bedroom. For one, none of my posters are on the wall. No Weezer. No Radiohead. No Michael Jordan. In fact, this room is three times the size of my bedroom. A large oak vanity sits in the far corner with an ironing board next to it. And the 47" TV (pure speculation) mounted on the wall by the door is hard to miss. Definitely not my bedroom.

But it's not Jessica's either. We've had make-out sessions in the pink slanted-ceiling, bunk-bedded room she shares with her twelve-year-old sister, and this isn't that room.

I need to get up. I skillfully roll the sleeping little princess off my chest and onto the bed. Her curls dangle carelessly over her eyelids as her mouth drops open and lets out a cute snore.

I walk back into the bathroom, stealthily closing the door behind me. I fumble for the light switch.

The bathroom is half the size of the bedroom, which is to say it is awfully large. A claw-foot bathtub sits at the far end, a two-headed shower nearly the size of the boys' locker room adjacent to it. I am greeted by the scent of lavender and rose, thankfully not the stench of sweaty undergarments and urine. The beige and slate-grey floor tiles feel cool to my naked feet. Two spacious walk-in closets flank the room. I allow my jaw to drop and then turn towards the sinks, the one on the right appearing to be mine, shaving cream and Old Spice deodorant dead giveaways. I let the faucet run for a few seconds before splashing cold water on my stubbled face.

I stand up straight and look into the mirror.

I am *not* eighteen years old.

Chapter 3

6:07 A.M.

Let's start with the good news. It is my face I'm looking at. Older, but no doubt that's my ugly mug. The fading scar across the bridge of my nose from that accident in Mr. Parker's rose garden at age six? Check. Big forehead? Check. Sure, there are a few more wrinkles, but that's my forehead. Big brown eyes, beautiful dark skin, chiseled chin . . . ok, so I like how I've aged. I take a moment to check out the rest of the package. Looks like I've been working out. Hot diggity dog.

I must be a personal fitness trainer. After all, I am a pretty good athlete—varsity track, tennis. But yesterday I was maybe a buck thirty, fully clothed. Today I look like I weigh 175, and there's not much body fat. I'm guessing I'm in my mid thirties.

I take my time in the shower, thoughts as misty as my surroundings. By habit, I finish my shower by turning the water to scalding hot so it feels like a million razor-sharp fingernails running down my back. I love the invigoration, the mix of pain and pleasure, for ten to fifteen seconds at most.

I step out of the shower and take a peek at my arms, abs, and pecs in the mirror again. I won't lie, I'm enjoying the older, super-fit me, maybe a little too much. With a towel wrapped around my waist, I step into my closet and flip the light switch. The walls are lined with suits and collared shirts. There's a hanger carrying dozens of neckties of various colors and designs. And then I see four long white coats hanging at the end of the rack. I tug one of the coats at the neck and peek at the breast pocket. "Benjamin Brew, MD. Adolescent Medicine."

My head is hurting again. *I'm a doctor? For teenagers?*

"Happy birthday, stud. Early Alzheimer's making it hard for you to pick out your clothes?"

I turn and there she is. The woman from the bed. *Not* Jessica.

This woman is drop dead gorgeous. Her tousled blond hair is the sexiest bedhead I have ever seen in my eighteen years on God's green earth. Hands on her hips, she stands before me, now partially clothed, draped in an oversized grey and yellow LA Lakers t-shirt. Wowsers.

"Why are you looking at me like that?" she asks innocently, though I catch a hint of playfulness in her voice. "It's too early for that and Kobi is still sleeping in our bed. You'll get your birthday fun later." She winks at me. I don't know what look I have on my face, but I'm hoping I can replicate it later.

I've never been past third base. And the beautiful woman in front of me says that will change tonight. But wait, I have been past third! I have a child—I think. I squeeze my eyes shut as pain needles my temple.

"You ok, Ben? You don't look so hot." *Is it that obvious?* "Why did you shower? You're not heading to the gym this morning?"

"I'm fine, just a little headache," I reply. "And, uh ... you look ... cute." That's the best I can do? I must have had better skills than that to have caught this fine woman's attention. *Step up your game, Brew, step it up!*

"Cute? I'll take that. You make me feel young again, talking like that. Keep it up ... cutie."

Now she's just mocking me, great. She walks towards me and plants a wet kiss on my lips. I try to linger but she's already turned around and is off to her closet, leaving me with closed eyes and parted lips.

I sigh and turn back to my clothes. I'm a doctor. I pick out doctor clothes and dress myself. Two-button grey-striped wool suit with a French-blue point collar dress shirt, black leather shoes. No tie. I pick out the starchiest white coat of the lot and toss it over my shoulder. In front of the bathroom mirror, I give myself a good once-over.

"Not bad for a forty-year-old doctor." My wife walks up behind me and puts her arms around my waist. *I'm forty? I'm practically a dinosaur!* My eighteen-year-old brain is having trouble processing all this. I need to figure out what the heck is going on! Asking the gorgeous blonde behind me seems logical, but I don't want to alarm her. If only I knew her name . . .

"So . . . uh . . . honey . . . what's for breakfast?" I use *honey* because that's what my dad used to call my mom. It feels awkward coming out of my mouth, and I'm glad she is still behind me and can't see the ridiculous, pathetic look on my face.

"Funny . . . *honey.* There's cereal in the pantry. Help yourself," she replies while gently rubbing my back. "The girls are expecting your usual Friday hot breakfast. You'd better get down there and whip something up."

Girls? Plural? I've been busy for the last twenty-two years. I think when I get downstairs I'm going to find out just how busy. My hope is less than five. I think I could handle four kids. I babysat the Thompson triplets three or four times without killing any of them (though I may have wanted to by the end of the night). I feel that buzzing pain in my ear again. The past is such a freaking blur! Better to focus on the present for now. My head seems to hurt less when I stay in the moment. I think I still know how to scramble eggs and microwave bacon.

Chapter 4

6:45 A.M.

I'm making breakfast and gosh darn, I'm doing a great job. The kitchen smells like Waffle House (my diner of choice), and my head feels better after a few slices of bacon. Everything *is* better with bacon, even headaches. I've used my amazing power of deduction to learn the names of my three (Yes! Only three!) girls. After watching them annoy each other for the last fifteen minutes, I've gathered that my oldest is Ana. She looks ten-ish. Next is Gabriella, a spunky almost-seven-year-old; I know this because her birthday is only weeks after mine, and she's reminded me of this fact twenty-four times in the last five minutes. And then the cutie still fast asleep upstairs in my bed? Kobi Lyn. She can't be more than three years old. And Kobi's not the only cute one—they're all adorable. Latte-brown skin, curly hair—my nameless wife's genes plus mine were a magical combination. I'm assuming I have a shotgun somewhere; no way I'm letting any boys near these girls.

They've already sung me "Happy Birthday" and threatened to give me forty spankings later tonight. Ana and Gabri have to catch a bus at the corner in ten minutes, and my wife is escorting them to the bus stop. I have *got* to figure out her name. She's already made fun of me for calling her honey, so I need to figure out her actual name because I can't avoid talking to her. It's funny—in your own house, there aren't labeled pictures of people like in a yearbook or museum. The only place to find names would be . . . oh . . . that's it . . . the mail. Or a wallet.

I yell out to no one in particular, "Have you seen my keys or wallet?"

"Same place they always are," Ana yells back from the kitchen table. Ana, clearly the smarty-pants of my daughters, points matter-of-factly towards a dresser in the kitchen nook. I clean my hands with a dishrag and walk over to a basket full of keys and wallets. I'm assuming the pink one is my wife's. Nope, Ana's. *She has a wallet? At age ten?* Her school ID has her birthday on the front.

I find my wife's wallet. Not pink, and definitely more sophisticated than Ana's. AMY CHRISTINA BREW. Amy Brew. Same age as me. Her birthday is in two months. That info might come in handy in a few weeks. Her driver's license hails from Texas. I really hope we don't live in Texas right now. I spend my childhood trying to get out of Alabama and I end up in Texas?

My wallet. I feel like I'm about to open a treasure box when Ana breaks my train of thought. "You having trouble finding your wallet, Dad, or are you 'borrowing' some dollars from me again without asking?" Apparently, my smart "guy" gene did not skip a generation. Well played, Ana.

I turn and give her my biggest grin. "I always pay you back, don't I?"

She's not fazed by my wink. "Sure, except for that one time. And the time before that. And the time before . . . you get the picture," she laments, shaking her head. "Parents. Sigh."

She is a sassy one, but I'm in love with her. Gabri is flipping through a magazine and shoveling down a spoonful of eggs. I feel the need to say something fatherly.

"Finish your breakfast, Gabri, the bus won't wait for you." She doesn't look up. Then her right thumb slowly lifts from her spoon and points straight up, her head barely nodding. Apparently I got through. *Yes!*

I take my wallet and keys and do what every guy does when he needs time to think: I find the nearest bathroom and lock myself in. In three short minutes, my world comes into focus. I am Benjamin Brew, DOB January 15, 1980. It is January 15, 2020. I know that because the tiny phone in my hand says so. This tiny phone is like a Nintendo Game Boy—on crack! I accidentally touch the screen and the phone starts to call someone named Angela. I hang up quickly—by touching the freaking screen! Imagine if I could play games on this device . . . if I am somehow dreaming, I am going to get freaking rich when I wake up, because this dream is full of some amazing futuristic ideas! *Back to the Future IV: Benjamin Brew reinvents the cordless phone. He then uses that phone to travel back to 1996 where things are normal. Michael J. Fox tags along as my quirky uncle, teaching me how to use protection so I don't become a teenage dad. I reveal my brilliant phone ideas, become the CEO of AT&T, and live a wealthy, happy life. I have kids when I am forty.*

I am really digging my wallet/phone combo. Mental note: Add wallet/phone to list of future patents and movie plot. I flip through my business cards and find my own. I am a doctor, and I work at the naval hospital in Portsmouth, Virginia. We are not in Texas. I also have a Texas driver's license, but why? I keep flipping through my wallet and find . . . a military ID. There's my picture. Retired Lieutenant Colonel Benjamin Brew. Aha! Something that makes sense! I was in the military. But the ID doesn't expire for another two years. That doesn't make sense. I definitely am no longer in the military, but I work at the military hospital? I find my hospital identification card. It states that I'm a member of the pediatrics department.

Commotion continues outside the bathroom. Someone's turned the TV on, and I can hear what sounds like a reporter in the middle of a breaking news segment. "—ina and US relations continue to sour. Last week's sinking of a Chinese freighter by a US submarine has increased tensions. The casualty count is up to thirty-seven. The US claims this freighter was involved in espionage off the coast of Japan, a claim vehemently denied by the Chinese. This on the heels of Chinese cyberattacks that brought down Wall Street for twenty-four hours this week, throwing the stock market into turmoil—attacks the US government have called an 'act of war.' Let's take you live to Beijing, where President Yu Qishan is holding a press conf—"

I hear the front door open. "Have a great birthday, Dad! See you at your party tonight!" Ana yells.

"Don't forget to wake up Kobi and get her to daycare! Your first patient's at eight," Amy adds.

I jump up in a panic. I didn't realize I had other responsibilities this morning! I flush the toilet because it seems like the right thing to do after being in the bathroom for so long. I run the tap for two seconds, then bolt out of the bathroom right as the front door closes. I sprint to the door and rip it open.

"Ames, can you take Kobi today? I need to get in to work early."

"Only because it's your birthday, BB. Next week you're nothing special. Just an old man." She winks at me.

I called her Ames and it worked! That just slipped out! I'm starting to feel more optimistic that I can continue this charade for a few more hours. I have no idea what I'm going to do tonight when I assume a bunch of people I won't recognize come over to my house to celebrate my fortieth. Yikes. I need to get to work. Maybe there, things will begin to make sense. I can lock myself in my office and figure out how to get back to the universe where I'm an eighteen-year-old high school senior with a steady girlfriend and plans to go to college.

Chapter 5

7:15 A.M.

I could get used to being a doctor. The black 2018 BMW Gran Coupe roars like a lion as I exit the driveway onto Summerhouse Lane. The voice-activated GPS has me on my way to the hospital, the turn-by-turn navigation displaying directly on the front windshield. Don't ask me how I figured out how to use all this technology—I didn't. I got in the car and pushed the On button. I placed my hands on the wheel and lamented, "How am I supposed to get to the naval hospital?" and then directions popped up on the windshield. Cars are way cooler in 2020. "I wonder if it can fly?" I'd whispered to myself, my giddy-meter going up to 11.

As I slowly pull out of the gated community (after a sightseeing excursion in and out of several cul-de-sacs with my mouth agape), I realize that I'm being followed. Actually, I've known since the minute I left the house. The grey four-door sedan fifty yards behind me was parked across the street, five houses down. During my neighborhood tour, it kept a healthy distance, matching my speed, timing its turns to keep me in sight.

Almost instinctively, I begin taking evasive measures, switching lanes haphazardly, running yellow lights, driving a bit unpredictably but not enough to be dangerous. The sedan matches my movements. I'm having fun. My dashboard display indicates there are several driving modes, including "Sport without

Dynamic Traction." I select this mode and break into a wide grin after gently tapping the accelerator and feeling the car lurch powerfully forward as if propelled by rockets. This may be the closest I get to driving KITT from *Knight Rider*, except that the onboard computer's voice reminding me to "proceed to the route" is decidedly feminine and not sarcastic. I slip the BMW into fifth and gun aggressively onto the onramp, the surge of the vehicle pressing my back into the leather seat. Apparently I learned stick shift sometime in the last twenty-two years. The sedan is trying to keep up but I'm good. I've increased the distance between us by another fifty yards, continuing my slick weave around the other morning commuters on I-64.

I see an opportunity to lose my pursuers. There's an opening in the wooded median about a quarter mile ahead. I cruise in the right lane at sixty MPH, waiting for my moment. In my side mirror, I see the grey sedan in the middle lane, gaining on me. The moment comes. I cut sharply into the middle lane, forcing a red Ford F-150 (with no kids inside it) to slam on his brakes. The back of my car fishtails to the right a bit, but that's intentional; the lack of dynamic traction places me perpendicular to the oncoming traffic. Now I just need to get past the left lane of cars . . . but that should be the easy part. The moment I decided to obstruct the pickup truck, I saw an eighteen-wheeler in the left lane reducing its speed and signaling to move to the middle to satisfy angry left-lane drivers wanting to pass. I downshift and slam on the gas, bursting past the barreling truck and its bellowing horn with plenty of room to spare. Within seconds, I'm through the wooded median and already in the left lane headed in the opposite direction. I can see through the trees to my left that there's a pileup, the honking cacophony confirming my success. The grey sedan won't bother me for the rest of the morning. The BMW adjusts my GPS route—I'll be at work in ten minutes. Right on time.

Chapter 6

7:55 A.M.

I have no idea where I learned to drive like that. I'm feeling a little bad that I've ruined the morning for quite a few people. But I was definitely being followed—and even though I don't know who they were, that sedan had government spook written all over it. I don't even know why I'm so sure—my infatuation with James Bond movies? Or my apparent military background?

I sheepishly show my ID to the hospital gate guard, afraid he'll somehow figure out that I'm an eighteen-year-old boy trapped in a forty-year-old's body. That I'm Ben Brew but not the Ben Brew on that ID card. I'm racking my brain, trying to remember if I attended the state fair last night and tangled with a fortune-telling, turban-wearing machine robot named Zoltar, when the guard waves me in. I drive around the parking garage for a frustrating six minutes; I finally find a spot on the highest deck, narrowly beating a uniformed sailor to it. He appears to be cursing me as I navigate between two minivans. I glance at the full van to my left, and for a split second I'm worried about the dent the six-year-old inside it is going to put in my car when his pencil-thin arms gleefully thrust the door open. But then something magical happens: his door smoothly *slides open*. The boy hops out with his twin sisters and the door slides shut on its own.

The future is amazing.

I follow signs from the parking lot to the hospital lobby. The coffee shop isn't Starbucks, but it looks like it'll do. A charming, heavily tattooed barista asks, "Your usual double shot, Doc?" and I nod and hand her two dollars even, like I've done this a million times. I'm hopeful the double shot will shake this headache, but this buzzing in my head feels special, beyond the reach of caffeine. I'm keenly aware now that it's not just my head that hurts, but my left ear, too. It feels achy, like a stubbed toe.

Without stopping to ask the front desk for directions, I march down the hall and take a sharp left before the pharmacy. I've guessed correctly: nestled in the back of the pediatrics clinic is an office with my name outside the door. My badge activates the lock and I'm in. I shut the door quietly behind me and lock it. Finally. Some alone time.

I sit down in my black swivel chair and immediately slip my ID into the card-reader slot on the keyboard. I'm no genius, just observant; I glanced into open offices on the way to my own. I'm hoping the computer doesn't ask me for a password. The technology of the future continues to amaze me—I follow the onscreen instructions and place my left thumb over the keyboard's fingerprint reader and my screen buzzes to life, cycling through startup windows and eventually settling onto a home screen. I've got nine unopened emails.

Those will have to wait. I open my internet browser and pray that AOL still exists—I suspect something far better and faster has taken its place. Something called Google pops up and appears to be a search window. I smile weakly as my stomach begins doing somersaults. Staring at the keyboard, I decide to type in the most logical search term: my name.

I read for the next ten minutes in complete silence. I'm not even sure I am breathing. This is what it must be like for someone with advanced Alzheimer's to be told who they are, what they've done, and not remember any of it. Graduated from Harvard magna cum laude, majored in cognitive neuroscience. Yale Medical School. Three-year pediatric residency at this hospital. Three-year fellowship in adolescent medicine. Then various jobs at different military hospitals. My headache is waning but as I try to remember these milestones of my career, the buzzing intensifies and my left ear burns.

I minimize the internet window because I need to clear my head for a moment. I begin scrolling through the emails. My eyes light on one from Angela Rogal. The subject is "Urgent." I'm about to open it when a loud knock interrupts me.

Oh no. Time to play doctor.

"Come in," I timidly offer. The handle jiggles and nothing happens. Oh right, it's locked. I roll over to the door and unlock it. The door swings open and a broad-shouldered black woman wearing a short white coat greets me.

"Hey, Dr. B! Happy birthday! You know I baked you a cake, but you can't have a slice until you see your morning patients. There's two waiting already. C'mon, honey, let's go."

While she's talking to me, I take a look at the badge on her lab coat: Grace. Grace Lively.

"Ok, Mrs. Grace, I'm ready to roll!" I try to sound eager.

She hands me two thick charts that I drop onto my desk with a soft thud. I open up the top one. Brianna Brock, eighteen years old. Chief complaint: anxiety. *Oh, Brianna, you have no idea.* My stomach is no longer doing somersaults—it's self-digesting as I walk towards Exam Room #1.

Chapter 7

Brianna is actually doing really well. I guess I knew what I was doing at her last appointment. I increased her Celexa, an SSRI, from 20 mg to 40 mg. This Google thing is amazing, because I now know what Celexa is and that SSRI stands for selective serotonin reuptake inhibitor. I've spent more time looking at the computer screen than at Brianna's face. She reports a huge decrease in panic attacks and palpitations. *Palpitations: rapid heartbeat* says Google . . . like my own right now as I ask Brianna questions about how she is feeling. I can't believe my luck—my first patient doesn't need brilliant medical decision-making. Just a refill. That doesn't stop me from feeling like a veritable Doogie Howser, MD, just slightly older . . . and not actually a genius. After a few minutes of clumsily working through her electronic medical record, I finally figure out how to give Brianna a one-month refill of her Celexa. I wish her good luck and send her on her way. One down. Only God knows how many to go. But honestly, how hard was it talking to another kid my age? Ok, not my actual age, my *brain* age. I can see myself falling in love with this job once I figure out where all the medical knowledge in my brain went.

I return to my office to look at the second chart Grace dropped in my lap. Carlos Lee. Focal segmental glomerulonephritis, adrenal insufficiency,

23

hypothyroidism, and moderate persistent asthma. I think the only word I recognize in his diagnosis list is "asthma." I'm in deep doogie—no, doo-doo. Sweat beads converge on my forehead as I grab the handle of Exam Room #2. No amount of Googlizing (is that a word?) Carlos's diagnoses would help me at this point; there's just no time. I can't cram ten years of medical training into five minutes of internet searching. I can always hope he's just here for a cold, right?

I open the door.

That ain't Carlos. Unless he's a slim, attractive, college-aged woman. Grace must have given me the wrong chart. The young lady in front of me looks healthy enough, so I'm hoping for an easy visit.

"I . . . uh . . . seem to have the wrong chart. I'm Dr. Brew. How can I help you today?"

"Really? You're going to act like you don't recognize me?" The annoyed look on the young woman's face sends me into a panic as I scan for clues to her identity. The oversized black fleece jacket she dons covers some of the letters on her silver Old Dominion University shirt. Her black jeans hide the tops of black boots, her legs crossed impertinently. Nope, there is nothing familiar about this person.

I nervously tug at my cuffs and stare blankly at the chart in my hands. This moment is exactly what I was afraid of. I knew I could only fake being a doctor for so long. Though I guess technically I'm not faking—I just don't remember how to be a doctor. And my problem right now isn't medical decision-making. It's facial recognition.

"Hey, cut me some slack, it's my fortieth birthday. I'm feeling a bit senile. Help me out."

The strawberry blonde doesn't miss a beat. "Stop messing with me. Why haven't you been answering my texts or calls?" she says angrily. She stands up, and we're now practically face to face.

Now I'm really starting to feel uncomfortable. Is this how medicine works these days? Patients call their doctors directly on their mobile phones? Seems a bit intimate to me. What's even more intimate is the fact that she's now in my personal space, scanning every inch of my face as if she somehow suspects I'm an imposter. Do I need to call security?

Instead of arguing with the young lady (and to break the lengthening uncomfortable silence), I decide to play along. I pull out my phone (though honestly, based on what I know of it so far, it's more like a portable computer) and take a look. I don't see any missed calls or "texts," as she calls them. I hold up my phone to show her and shake my head. She grabs it out of my hand—well, at least that's what I think she's going to do. She actually grabs both my phone and my hand, pressing my right thumb to the top left corner of my screen, holding it there for a full five seconds. I'm not sure why I let her. Then my phone does something weird. A new screen appears displaying a bunch of messages and missed calls. The mysterious teen now sports a matter-of-fact look on her face.

"What the hell is wrong with you, Brew? I don't care that it's your frickin' birthday. We've got less than fourteen hours before there's an 'international crisis on our hands'—yeah, those are your words, not mine—and you're in here playing doctor. And we kinda already have one international crisis that we're currently dealing with, so , geez, what's one more? What's our plan? I've been evading Gs all morning just to get here. I'm sure they know I'm here—after you IGNORED me, I had to try to guess what you'd do next." She's tapping her temple with her index finger. "Coming here was stupid. For both of us. I even emailed your civilian account. Let me guess—you didn't read that either." She sighs.

I'm trying to take in everything she has just said. I stare blankly.

"Well, don't just stand there. Unless you want this birthday to be your last day on God's green earth. Grab your bag and let's get the hell ou—"

And then the room goes black.

Chapter 8

8:43 A.M.

My 8:30 patient (I have no idea what else to call her at this point) grabs my wrist and pulls me towards the door. She opens it slightly and timidly peeks out into the hallway; over her shoulder, I can see it's strobing like the Anderson Roller Skating Rink from my twelfth birthday. Only one kid seized.

"This is your office—what's the best way out of here?" she asks, barely turning to look back at me.

I'm paralyzed, a deer caught in the strobe lights. "Wh—, wh—, what's your name?" is all I can muster. Knowing her name might not save my life at this moment, but dammit, I need to start somewhere.

"Seriously, Brew? Angela Rogal, nice to meet you. Now can we get the freak out of here before the Gs get here?"

Angela. Ok, doesn't ring a bell, but she seems to know me fairly well and wants to help. God knows I need all the help I can get right now. And she is clearly not one of my patients. I toss Carlos's chart onto the examination table and follow Angela into the hallway. There is no need to go back to my office, my phone/wallet is glued to my left hand (I'm convinced if I hang onto it long enough it will accidentally slap some sense into me). I start a brisk walk down the hallway towards the receptionist's desks, then almost mow Angela over as I do an abrupt about-face and start moving to the back of the clinic.

"There's a back exit this way. Not sure how I know that, but I think it's right around the corner."

And there it is. We bypass the elevator and jog down two flights of steps. Emergency lights are still flashing. The overhead intercom reports a Code Black. That doesn't sound good.

Angela can see the panic in my face and stops me in the crosswalk to the parking deck. "That's an intruder alert, Brew. Which means very soon the entire facility will be on lockdown." She stares deep into my eyes. "Which means we'll be trapped in here with whoever is coming for you."

Who is after me? I taste bile in my mouth and feel lightheaded. It takes me several seconds to remember where I parked the BMW. "My car . . . fifth floor" is all I can muster.

"No, let's take mine, I parked in a dirt lot over by the west gate." I helplessly follow her to the back side of the hospital, alarm sirens bellowing around us. She pushes her car remote and the parking lights on a little blue . . . Prius? . . . light up.

"Get in the back, we don't have a lot of time." I'm grateful that she's offering to drive; my nerves are a bit frazzled. I open up the back door on the passenger's side. I'm halfway into the car when Angela yells, "Hey! WTF? Get in the back! The trunk! I can't sneak you out if you're waving at the guard as we pull out!"

Thankfully the trunk is bigger than it looks from the outside. The hatchback has a slightly opaque window so I pull a large wool blanket over my head and lie still. The car almost silently hums into gear— I wouldn't have known we were moving if not for the sound of gravel crunching beneath the tires. I feel every bump as we peel out of the parking lot. My spatial sense is pretty good—I can tell when we've gotten through the gate and are back on the main road. I pull off the blanket and bang on the backseat.

One minute later, the Prius pulls to a stop and the trunk opens. "Patience, buddy. No point in sneaking you out and then getting nabbed right out of the gate."

But I'm beyond patience. We're standing on the side of the road next to a KFC. A homeless man pushes a cart in the middle of the street a few feet away from us. I have no idea where I am other than Portsmouth, Virginia. I have no idea who is chasing me. And I don't know who Angela is or who she thinks I am. But she knows my name and thinks I am in danger. I need to tell her the truth—which is that I don't know what the hell is going on today.

"Angela, I woke up this morning with . . . amnesia. But not like the 'I forgot my name' type amnesia. More of the 'What happened over the last twenty-two years of my life' kind of memory loss. I imagine this is what a really, reeeally bad hangover feels like. Not that I'd know. Since last night I went to bed as a relatively alcohol-naïve seventeen-year-old looking forward to his eighteenth birthday." I pause dramatically to allow Angela's brain to catch up to her face. Wait for it . . . wait for it . . . success! Now that I have her looking like Shaggy at the climax of a *Scooby-Doo* episode, I feel like she is finally feeling my pain. Maybe not feeling, but possibly, just possibly, using her youthful brain to imagine the fear I've felt all day. *Terrifying*, her face says. Yes, that's exactly what I'm trying to convey.

"Today I wake up on my fortieth birthday. I have a rip-roaring headache and my left ear hurts. I have a wife . . . A WIFE! And kids? I played along this morning and tried to go about business as usual. Business as usual being a doctor, I guess? And then you show up to my office and tell me to stop playing doctor because I'm in danger and I get into the trunk of a car and sneak off of a military installation during a lockdown. So while I'm not feeling super patient, I am kind of eager to start feeling like myself again . . . so how about we cut through the bullshit and right to the truth."

I finish that last statement without hiding my anger and frustration. I'm still wearing my doctor's coat, and I reach into the breast pocket and pull out a cigarette. I start patting my pants for a lighter, but Angela is already moving towards me, lit lighter cradled in her palms.

"You really do need to kick this habit," she says, her voice quivering, clearly bothered by the verbal diarrhea I just dumped into her mental latrine. "We're not exactly helping each other quit."

It's only then, in the midst of lighting up, that I realize what's just happened. Apparently, I'm a smoker. *Goddamn, what other bad habits have I acquired over the last two decades?* Apparently, I'm also a potty mouth.

"Look, Brew, I don't know what's gotten into you. You were perfectly normal yesterday." She's pacing and running her hands through her hair; now *I* look like the sane one. "Ok, 'perfectly' may be an exaggeration. You did morning clinic, then we met for afternoon casework. You had a meeting with the director that you were pretty torn up about. We talked it out. You said you'd sleep on it and we'd talk in the morning. But you said some pretty disturbing things—things I thought might get you, and by you I mean us—in quite a bit of deep doo-doo. So I wanted to check on you last night but you didn't answer my calls or texts. I figured you were getting some early birthday action, but then you didn't respond this morning, either. So I tracked you down at work and here we are."

I'm still blushing (she can't tell) as Angela plucks the cigarette out of my mouth and takes a long drag. She doesn't give it back. "So you don't remember the last two decades of your life, eh? You don't remember joining the agency, special-ops training, playing doctor for the president of the United States' daughter? You don't remember the crazy story you told me last night about a microchip that was implanted in her ear that's messing with her memory? This better be some sick joke, Brew. If not, we're hosed."

Chapter 9

9:12 A.M.

I don't think I like the person I've become. The smoking and foul language are less than attractive. But I think those are fixable behaviors. Being some sort of special agent? I apparently made that choice and now I'm in some kind of mess. It explains why I'm really fit. Working for the president? Ah, maybe smoking is how I cope with being at the beck and call of the president's (demanding, I can only imagine) daughter. But there's a lot of stuff I still don't understand. Angela has some explaining to do.

We're back in her car now and driving down the freeway. I'm driving; it's helping me clear my head. Sort of. Angela explains this "hybrid" car will sometimes feel funny because the battery takes over the gasoline engine to power the motor . . . weird. Definitely didn't have these in 1998.

I don't really know where I'm going but I'm driving in the direction of my house. It's been about ten minutes and I haven't stopped asking questions. And I've finally gotten some answers, not that I'm feeling any better.

"So . . . *partner* . . . thanks for catching me up on the last two years of my life. Sort of. I don't share much, do I?"

"Well, you tell me . . . would your wife find it a little strange if you were hanging out with a nineteen-year-old college student all the time *after* you left the clinic? Plus you're kind of old enough to be my dad. We have more of a . . . father-daughter relationship." Her pause makes me think she's not telling the whole truth. Maybe it's the way she's looking at me as she speaks, in a way that a daughter definitely does *not* look at her father. "Ok, that sounds a little awkward," she clarifies. "Maybe sensei-student is more accurate."

I smirk. "Good point about the wife. So she doesn't know about you?" Angela shook her head. "Well, that's probably good. Does she know that I'm a trained killer?" I ask, flashing my most debonair Pierce Brosnan/James Bond/*GoldenEye* smile.

"Ha, ha. You're hot stuff, Brew, but I wouldn't call you a killer. You're a pudding pop. A softie," says Angela, sticking out her bottom lip and fluttering her eyelids. "But if my life was in danger, I'd want you coming to save me. Hell, the president handpicked you for his daughter, so you must have done something right. That's something you've never told me—how you got picked for this job as her personal doctor and occasional bodyguard."

I scratch my head. "I'd tell you now if I could remember. Or maybe there's a good reason I never told you. Speaking of doing something right—you're the one who gets to hang with the First Daughter every day," I say, trying to turn the conversation back to Angela's life, since thinking about the details of mine make my head buzz. "Huh . . . is it hard for you, faking friendship with the president's daughter? Carrie—that's her name, right? I don't mean for that to sound bad."

"Wow . . . that does sound bad. Good to see you still have a way with words." Before I can apologize, she continues. "I'm not a fake friend. I'm really close to Carrie now . . . but as an agent my job is to protect her and keep her out of trouble."

"Please forgive my ignorant comments," I say. Given the way my brain is functioning today, the comments are literally ignorant: lacking knowledge or information. *I've been studying for my SAT recently, haven't I?* I laugh internally, doing my best to suppress a grin. I am physically older than Angela, but mentally, I'm her junior. Best not to actually articulate that to her, or I might never live it down.

"No offense taken, Brew. I know what you meant. I'm just sensitive about our friendship," she says, fidgeting in her seat. "The director told me the president is adamant that I spend more time with Carrie to keep her in line. And recently, she's been listening to me more, but apparently still hanging out with some bad apples when I'm not around. But I just can't physically be with her ALL the time. Even when we're split into different class sections, I always do my best to get reassigned to hers." She turns her gaze to the window, and in its reflection I see her pained visage. "The hard part is Carrie doesn't know a major reason why I'm so close to her is because I'm paid to be. If she ever found out, I don't know how I'd live with myself.

It's already hard making friends outside of school with this job. I am not your typical college student."

"Oh, sure you are. Bodyguarding government-agent college kids are a dime a dozen. Are you really just nineteen?" I ask incredulously, desperately trying to lighten the mood.

"No, old man, I turned twenty a few weeks ago, but I'm guessing you forgot taking me out for my birthday. And by taking me out, I mean you took me to Starbucks and bought me a grande iced Oprah Chai with whip. And a slice of pumpkin bread. Big spender." She draws out the "i" in *big.*

I know Angela cannot see me blushing but I am embarrassed by my apparent lack of sensitivity. And immaturity. Saying the word "big" in my presence today simply invokes images of Tom Hanks dancing on a foot piano, and suppressing my giggles has been quite the challenge all morning. *Grow up, Brew!* So I say the first thing that comes to mind. "Well, it's not like it was your twenty-first. You could have gotten a venti and *two* slices of pumpkin bread."

Angela nods slowly in acknowledgment of my poor attempt at humor. "Thanks, jerk."

I change the subject. "So you signed up for this jo—"

"Job at eighteen because the benefits were out of this world. Tuition paid for. Awesome physical training. Hazard pay. And for this short four-year assignment, I get a small paycheck for the rest of my life and my pick of jobs or grad schools after this. Kinda hard to beat."

I stare at Angela with respect. A gutsy decision for a young woman with obviously a great deal of moxie. High risk, high reward. "Yeah, I wouldn't have been able to turn a sweet deal like that down at your age." And as I say those words, I really mean them, since I *feel* like I'm her age but I know I'm not. We're about a mile from the house so I pull the car onto the shoulder of the freeway.

"Listen, Angela, this has been quite the day already. Thanks for helping me out in more ways than one. I think the key to what's happening to me must be yesterday. Can you tell me more about the crazy stuff I was telling you about yesterday? My meeting with the . . . director?"

Her face goes blank as she leans her cheek against her window. She lets out a sigh.

"Brew . . . it was weird. You had a 1300 meeting with the director. It was supposed to be short, like fifteen minutes. We were going to debrief on Carrie right after that, talk about her medication compliance, her most recent seizure, her apparent drug problem— you didn't end up calling me until 1415. When we met up at Starbucks, you looked pissed. Didn't seem like you were listening to me at all. You kept apologizing for being distracted. When I finally asked you how your meeting went . . ." She pauses and turns to look out her window. She lightly bangs her forehead on the glass. "You totally lost it. I've never seen you like that before.

You said . . . you said the agency had been implanting microchips into soldiers and agents for some time. Chips that could selectively erase parts of memory. So . . . this isn't a joke? Did the agency wipe *your* memory?"

Chapter 10

9:27 A.M.

I'm listening in disbelief. This can't be happening. Twenty-two years of my life, gone? I don't remember graduating college or medical school. I don't remember meeting Amy or getting married. I don't remember the births of my children. Tears well up in my eyes, but my hands are glued to the steering wheel. It dawns on me that I may never get those memories back if what Angela is saying is true.

I think back to the Fisher-Price tape recorder I used to carry around everywhere when I was a child. Side A of the cassette that came with it relayed a silly story about a pet rhino—at the end of the story, the listener was encouraged to flip the tape over and record their own silly story. I'd recorded and re-recorded myself singing, laughing, harassing my older brother, about a hundred times on Side B of that tape. Until the day I forgot to flip the tape and recorded over Side A. I was crushed. I ran to my dad and asked him how to undo my mistake, to bring back the rhino story. Surely there was some way. My dad simply shook his head and handed me back the faded cassette. "It's gone," he said. That didn't stop me—I was a seven-year-old with dogged determination; there was no such thing as an unfixable mistake. I listened to Side A over and over again, hoping that somehow underneath the murky sounds of my recorded giggles, the original recording remained, and that somehow I could reverse the damage I had done.

I grit my teeth and look at myself in the rearview mirror. *No.* If there's a chance I can get my memories back, even if it means declaring war on the agency, whoever they are, they are going to have their hands full with me. Those memories belong to me. No one should have the power to take them away.

"Angela, will you help me? Get my memory back? I need to know what happened yesterday. And it's not like I can just walk into the agency and ask them why they did this to me."

She still has her forehead pressed against her window. In the reflection, I can see her eyes are closed.

"Brew, I don't know. I could get into so much trouble. I . . . I need to tell you someth—"

Intense vibrations and the plucking of a country fiddle interrupt our conversation. It takes me a few seconds to realize these rumblings and sounds are originating from my phone. Was there a problem with the classic "brrring" sound? I fumble in my pocket and peek at the screen: one missed call from Amy twenty minutes ago, probably when I was in the trunk and lying on top of my phone. The caller ID says "Chang, Jang-Ho." I ignore the call.

"Who was that?" Angela asks eagerly.

"Really, Angela? Unless the caller ID says 'wife,' I'm pretty sure I'm not going to know who is calling. Someone named Chang."

My phone is hee-hawing again. Chang didn't leave a message the first time. My left ear is aching and my head buzzing. I ignore Chang again.

Angela turns to face me. "Maybe you shouldn't answer your phone until we figure out what is going on. Maybe it's not such a bad idea to go into the agency and just turn yourself in. Maybe they'll just explain why they did it. Maybe they can give you your memory back."

I look at her quizzically. "I may have lost my memory, but I'm not naïve. You really think if they went to such great lengths to wipe my memory that they'll just welcome me back with open arms? C'mon."

She averts her eyes. Why would she suggest something so stupid after sneaking me out of the hospital?

The car shakes a little as the highway traffic whips past. My phone rings for a third time. I'm sure it's Chang. I decide to reward his persistence, assuming I can at least fake my way through a thirty-second phone call. Maybe it's my massage therapist reminding me of an appointment.

I timidly raise the phone to my ear. "Hello?"

"Benjamin, it's Jang-Ho. Are you ok? Have you been confused at all today or feeling like you've forgotten things you should know?"

I don't know how the person on the other line could possibly know how my day was going. I'm about to hang up out of fear. Is this some agency trick?

"I know this sounds strange, but please hear me out," he continues. "You warned me yesterday this might happen and you asked me to call and check on you today. You're in danger and we need to meet. Are you alone? Wait, don't answer that. You can't trust anybody right now, not even Angela. Drive to 500 Shoreline Road and I'll explain everything. Come alone if you can. If you don't believe you can trust me, I know your left ear is hurting. It's the microchip that *we* designed causing your ear pain and disrupting your memory, Ben. You're not crazy. Come quickly."

Chapter 11

9:37 A.M.

I can't look Angela in the eye as the line goes dead. I stare straight ahead. She's looking at me expectantly, as if I'm going to tell her what was being said during the phone call.

I push the Prius's ignition button and wait for the gentle hum of the engine. Stepping firmly on the accelerator, I bring the car up to speed and merge onto the highway. I still haven't said a word, lost in a whirlwind of thought. Angela breaks the silence.

"I'm guessing 'Chang' said something important. Care to share, partner?"

My instinct is telling me that everything Chang said is true. Especially the part about not trusting anybody, even Angela. Her comment about returning to the agency didn't strike me as particularly savvy, either. I need to be careful.

"Angela, I need to borrow your car and go somewhere. Alone. A place where I'll get some answers."

"Seriously, Brew? What are you going to do? Leave me on the side of the road to hitchhike home? Let's go,

I'll plug in the address. I'm still your partner, no matter what the voice on the other end of that line said."

I shake my head at her. "Angela, it's not personal. I think you could be in danger because of something I've done. It's safer for you to distance yourself from me until I sort this out."

I take the next exit and pull into a Chevron. "Call a cab. Get somebody from the agency to pick you up. This is for the best."

"After all these years, you're going to dump me like this? Oh wait, you don't remember anything I've ever done for you. You suck, Brew." She reaches into her coat pocket and pulls out her phone, a replica of mine. "Fine, I'll call a cab while you get my shit out of the trunk."

I feel terrible for having to do this to her, but I know Chang is right. Angela begins to dial a number into her phone as I turn to open my door. In my window's reflection, I catch a glimpse of her raised right arm and instinctively jerk my head backwards into her face. The sound of her nose crunching is sickening but I don't have time to think about that. I twist in my seat to face her and her nails scrape my right cheek. I wince but keep my eyes open. Her bloody nose isn't slowing her down, and the syringe in her right hand is dripping. She makes another lunge at my neck but I parry with my left forearm. It's my turn to attack, and I launch myself at her, my right arm extended to pin her against her door. But she's limber, lifting her knees to her chest and in

43

one smooth motion thrusting her boots into my midsection.

She knocks the wind out of me, but the momentum of my 180-pound frame won't be stopped. I ignore the pain and push through, grabbing her by the neck with my right hand, my left hand clutching her right. She's determined to sink that needle into me.

I have other ideas. With a quick twist of my left hand, I redirect the needle towards her outstretched left arm, the one trying to prevent me from squeezing her neck. Her nose is bloodied, defeat plastered on her face, and I want to show mercy but can't—she watches helplessly as I force her to plunge the needle into her own antecubital fossa. *Ante-what?* "Veiny inner elbow area" rolls off the tongue much easier, but I guess deep down my mind does remember some medical stuff. I'm as careful and delicate as I can be, mouthing the words "I'm sorry" as she drifts into unconsciousness.

As I prop her limp body against the passenger door, I think about what might have happened if . . . if she'd actually drugged me. Where would I have woken up? Would I have? What would happen to Amy and the kids? I guess I'm glad this memory loss didn't wipe out skills like self-defense and intuition. Otherwise it'd already be game over.

I wipe the blood from my cheek with the back of my hand and slowly grip the cold steering wheel.

Chang is waiting for me.

Chapter 12

9:57 A.M.

Twenty minutes later, I pull in to the address Chang gave me with high expectations. He must have answers. I spoke to him yesterday. He knows why my head and ear are aching. But what if this is just another trap? It can't be. Angela, my real partner or not, is working with the enemy. And given how I handled her, I feel more confident in my abilities to overcome adversity. I wonder what other hidden talents I have. *"What if I'm a ninja?"* I whisper to myself. Damn . . . there goes my teenage brain drifting off again. I need to stay focused on the matter at hand . . . I need to figure out who my friends and enemies are.

I sincerely hope Chang is one of the good guys.

A six-foot, middle-aged Asian man is standing in the door of a two-story condo, his arms folded across his chest. He wears a long-sleeved white shirt, faded blue jeans, and jet-black cowboy boots. *Did I miss my exit and land in Texas? Though I guess Chang's appearance somewhat explains my country-fied mobile phone ring— was my phone trying to warn me?* Once I'm done staring at him from the comfort of the parked vehicle, I crack open my door and place a foot on the pavement before remembering that I can't leave Angela in the car. I have no idea how long she'll be out, so I decide to bring her inside with me. As awkward as it might be to carry a grown woman over my shoulder in broad daylight, I have no choice. She looks no more than 125 pounds, but limp bodies always feel heavier than they should (I know this from babysitting seven-year-old Cayley Stoekl two nights ago), so I'm huffing a bit when I approach the door. Chang doesn't look at all surprised. Not even amused.

"Good idea. We should question her when she comes around," he says without a greeting. He closes the door behind me. I lay Angela on a red microfiber couch in the living room. The condo is sparsely furnished. An upright mahogany Steinway rests against the wall, loose sheets of music strewn on the bench. An adjacent wall sports a lonely crimson Harvard banner hanging at eye level. I see no family photos, no evidence of a significant other or kids. A glass sliding door at the back of the room lets in soft natural light. When I complete my quick visual inspection and turn around, Chang is staring at me urgently.

"I don't know how much time we have so I'll get right to it. By now you must realize that there is a microchip in your left ear that is blocking your ability to remember anything between this morning when you woke up and . . . "

I finish his sentence. "The night before my eighteenth birthday."

"Wow . . . that's a larger memory gap than I expected. You must have one of the first gens." He begins pacing anxiously. "First-generation chips. Let me guess . . . every time you try to remember a specific event during the last twenty-two years, your ear hurts worse. That was a glitch we . . . *I* never figured out how to fix in the first-generation MemSave chip. But you did."

"You're joking, right?" I plead, knowing deep down that Chang either speaks the truth or is a willing participant in the most elaborate prank my brother has every played on me. "We designed this chip?" I point at my chest, then his, then mine, then his, until I get tired of pointing.

"Yes, Benjamin, *we* did. Truthfully, I designed the 1.0 and you helped me create the 1.1 and 1.2. So I know that one of the glitches of the 1.0 is the massive headache and buzzing when it's activated. I thought you'd fixed that in the 1.2 chip by tinkering with the ohmmeter settings."

I stifle another laugh, but this isn't really funny. I hope it's obvious to Chang that I'm having trouble taking this in. "When you came to my Massachusetts General Hospital lab as a freshman at Harvard, I knew you were bright. You were a cognitive neuroscience major, so my Center for Neurodegenerative Disorders was the perfect place for you to complete a thesis. I had completed the first-gen chip, version 1.0, about two years prior. In pilot testing it had minimal success. The idea had been to preserve the memories of individuals suffering from Alzheimer's, Parkinson's, or other conditions leading to dementia. As an individual lost his or her memory, the chip would take memories formed after implantation and loop them—hence the individual would never truly lose his memories—almost like a neuronal scrapbook on repeat in the brain. But in testing we found a glitch: that in addition to preserving memories, we could actually erase them. Not very selectively, but nonetheless large chunks of time. Weeks, even months. A friend in the air force heard about my research and got me a grant. They didn't know how exactly my chip would be useful, but they wanted to immediately begin testing."

It's a strange sensation to hear someone tell you about something you did, in great detail, and not remember doing it. But I'm taking it all in. I'm trying not to overthink it, since Chang has me convinced it might make my head hurt worse.

"So you put this chip in my ear?"

He shakes his head, exasperated. "Benjamin, I had no idea you had a first-gen MemSave chip in your ear. Something happened yesterday that made you suspect you might be chipped. Like you told me yesterday, you must have gotten it around your eighteenth birthday. Try to remember that day."

Chang busies himself at the dining room table while I steady myself on the edge of the couch and attempt to recount that day. It isn't hard to do, because it feels like yesterday.

I was at the air force recruitment office in Birmingham completing the last of my ROTC signup requirements. After the mandatory physical exam, Staff Sergeant Gomes took me into another room and told me I needed screening lab work and immunizations, standard stuff. I needed to sign a waiver first, and he told me to sign it quickly because there was another recruit right behind me. I glanced over the paperwork— I'm usually pretty anal about reading things like that, but it was unusually long. I signed my name to the bottom and the air force medic taking care of me promptly drew my blood and gave me two shots. Nothing in my ear. I knew I was going to have to come back the next day, on my birthday, to sign the official paperwork. I went home and celebrated with my parents over sparkling grape juice, their faces full of pride at the thought of their son joining the military ranks. We agreed not to party too hard since my birthday celebration would be the next day. Sparkling grape juice and cheering aside, I remember lying in bed that night worried that perhaps I had signed away too much of my freedom at such a young age.

I curse under my breath,, shaking my head in dismay. "I still don't remember getting ... chipped. Nothing strange happened that day."

"Yes, Benjamin," Chang starts, his voice full of reassurance. "You told me this whole story yesterday over the phone." He pauses. "In a different context. You lamented the lost innocence of your young civilian client, that the two of you were not much different. Teenagers who had lost their freedom. Yours, voluntarily. Hers? Not so much. The implanted chip has taken away her ability to control her behavior. She's behaving erratically, you've said. I don't have the security clearance, but from what I can gather, your client is fairly pretty high profile.

"Remember when we first suspected the military had been using our chip without our authorization?" Chang swivels his head to look at me, his face eager, then suddenly blank. "Ok, that was a dumb question— of course you don't. Back when you were still working in my lab as an undergrad, you knew I had already given up on the 1.0. We were working on the 1.2 when we stumbled upon the memory-deleting abilities. So our focus changed; we dubbed it the second-generation chip, 2.0, and you had bold ideas about what the uses could be in humans. We had only tested mice, of course. We weren't ready to use human subjects, but the military kept pushing us. We did a presentation before the joint chiefs pitching our chip as a potential cure for PTSD. Soldier returns from the field having experienced scarring events? Simply erase the memory of the deployment." Chang speaks with his back facing me, his hands busy with something at the table.

"But Chang, how is any of this ethical? What if the soldier *wanted* to live with his choices, the memories of his military service? Uncle Sam can't decide that for him. I'm not even sure how to address the civilian side of things, but my guess is that it's illegal. What business did we have playing God?"

Chang looks over his shoulder, his face strained. "Conversations we had over several hours and over many beers and cups of coffee, Benjamin. It's good to see the chip doesn't erase morality. These were your exact concerns—even as a young college and medical student. And mine as well. We demanded the chip, if it ever reached human testing, be implanted completely voluntarily, with full disclosure."

I arch my eyebrows as my heart beats faster. "I'm waiting for the 'but.'"

Chang sighs and cocks his head up, his thin black hair flopping backwards. "But . . . you and I . . . had a falling out, of sorts. I wanted nothing to do with human testing because it seemed dangerous. I left the project but you stayed on board, even after medical school, emailing updates from time to time. Sounds like you had great success with the chip . . . you mentioned 'Nobel Prize' a few times."

I laugh out loud. Loudly. I take a peek at Angela to see if my guffaws have awoken her. Her eyes remain shut and her breathing is slow and steady. I can't believe the cojones on me. *Really, Ben? Nobel Prize?*

Chang presses on despite my ongoing giggles, his voice becoming more serious. "But then recently, I gather, you went snooping and found that the agency had been implanting chips—even first-gen ones—involuntarily for several years in not just soldiers, but civilians as well. That's when you snapped. Sure, you were making huge strides in treating PTSD. But how could you go to press with the results when the basic standards of full disclosure had been violated? When you called me yesterday, you wanted to go to the press. But then you suspected you had a chip and knew the risks. I told you not to confront the director, but you did anyway. It didn't go well. So you frantically left me a voicemail—from a payphone or from some number I didn't recognize—and you told me that if you seemed like you had lost your memory, then it was true. You asked me to . . . to . . . " Chang's voice trailed off.

"What did I ask you to do, Chang?"

He turns away from the dining table and the glint of a scalpel catches my eye. I freeze.

"You asked me to cut off your ear."

Chapter 13

It makes sense. Of course I asked him to cut off my ear. How else could I deactivate the chip? And if I was going to stop the agency, right these wrongs, I would need my full faculties. Now obviously I could have done this myself yesterday, without involving Chang. But my guess is I wasn't really sure if 1) I had a chip in my ear, as they are incredibly small, 2) what ear the chip was in (what if I cut the wrong ear?), and 3) what if they didn't even activate the chip? What if the agency was willing to consider my concerns and have an honest conversation? Cutting off my ear preemptively? A tad aggressive, methinks.

Well, I think all those questions have been answered. I have a chip. It's in my left ear. And the agency wants me to forget about my concerns. Whoever is calling the shots—the director, or whoever is above him—isn't very bright. I'm not sure what they expected to happen when they erased ALL my memories from the past twenty-two years. Maybe they hoped I would go into a vegetative state? Be committed to a mental facility after having a psychotic break? Plan might have worked, had I not seen it coming. Seems as if they underestimated the co-creators of the chip. Speaking of which . . .

"So, Chang ... why cut my ear off? Isn't there another fail-safe?" I ask, my voice brimming with hope.

"Short of breaking into the agency mainframe?" Chang crushes my hope with a shake of his head. "Not that I know of. Remember, when we were still working together, our only subjects had been mice."

"Well, I guess that leaves me no choi—"

"Wait!" It's Angela. She sits up on the couch, her hands still bound with twine I borrowed from Chang's garage. The crusted blood under her nose gives her a grizzled appearance. She still looks snowed by whatever was in the syringe.

"I ... I heard everything. Brew, I'm so sorry. I made a terrible mistake." Her slurred words are becoming clearer. "Is it really true about the chip? Do you think I have one, too?"

I hadn't really thought about that. Something tells me that if I had my memory back I'd know.

"I don't know, Angela. But there's a good chance that you do, based on what I told Chang yesterday." Knowing someone could possess that kind of control, brain-memory-erasing control, is, well, frightening. At any moment, memories could be taken away. And the scary thing is? We wouldn't even know. How can I know Angela's memory hasn't already been tampered with?

I clap my hands and shake them solemnly. "I think our best recourse is to remove the chip in my ear ...

now. At least I'll know why the agency is coming after me, and I can come up with a plan to stop them. I hope. But it's my only chance."

"Our only chance," Angela pleads. "I know I tried to drug you, Brew, but I was just acting under orders. The director . . . he said . . . he said awful things about you. That you'd gone rogue. That you were a national-security risk and that we needed to know how much you knew. He said he thought you were on drugs or had a psychotic break so I needed to proceed with caution. Then you called and told me about the chip in Carrie and I really thought you were crazy. Now I know he was lying, and I'm pissed." The glazed look clearing from her face, Angela looks more like herself now. "So, any chance I can get you to cut this twine, Chang?"

I'm standing behind the couch now, and Chang looks at me, as if to seek my approval. I give him a cautious nod, and he nods back. Scalpel in hand, he gingerly steps towards a seated Angela and grabs her bound wrists.

"And Brew, I'm the one who should be sorry," she says over her shoulder. I should have trusted you. I should ha—oh shit." Angela dramatically pauses, the blood draining from her face as she looks towards her jacket pocket. "My phone. We've gotta get the f—"

And then the condo windows shatter into thousands of tiny little pieces as the sound of gunfire and breaking glass fills the room.

Chapter 14

10:22 A.M.

I can't hear anything. All I can see of Chang is his bloodied shirt that matches the color of the furniture he now drapes. I crouch behind the couch and his limp body; Angela is beside me, having alertly flipped over the back of the couch as chaos ensued. I wasn't hit, and by the looks of it neither was she.

The gunfire has stopped for now, I think, because I don't see couch fuzz or glass shards flying everywhere. Chang's scalpel, blade down, pokes up from the beige carpet about four feet away from us, about halfway between us and the dining table. Angela and I see it at the same time. My instinct is to knock her out while her hands are still tied—she'd be one less agent for me to deal with while trying to extricate myself from this situation. *Extricate . . . thanks again, SAT prep.* Angela grabs my sleeve, her desperate eyes trying to make contact with mine.

"Brew, it's not what you think," she shouts, panicked. I'm pleased that my hearing has returned. "Listen to me, we don't have much time! Cut my twine . . . if we're going to get out of this you need my help. That tactical team is going to be in here in less than ninety seconds. Yes, they are here because . . . because I called them. When I was 'calling a cab,' I was activating a tactical response team . . . it's probably just Johnson and Holley, they're my assigned backup today. They followed me here—but that was activated before I knew the truth. You can't get out of here without my help! Trust me!"

She's right. I need her. And the only person I can trust is bleeding out on the couch behind me. I drag the scalpel closer to us with my foot, not wanting to expose my body to whoever has a gun trained on this room. Before I cut the twine, I look one last time into Angela's eyes. And I trust her.

Chapter 15

10:24 A.M.

I'm sitting in a dining room chair with my back to the door. My head is bowed. My hands are tied behind my back.

I may have made a terrible mistake.

I can hear Angela opening the front door, but I can't make out the conversation so I'm even more nervous. I hear footsteps approaching. I close my eyes and calm my breathing. For a second, I realize that two minutes ago someone was about to cut off part of my ear. How quickly things change.

I hear and smell the two agents as they approach. Their footsteps are heavy. The one approaching from my right must be heavyset, I'd guess 230 pounds. He reeks of sweat and cologne. The one on the left has an exaggerated limp and is grunting, so I'm guessing his injury is recent. He had something with barbecue for lunch, probably stopped at the Joe's BBQ I passed a mile down the road to grab a bite before their stakeout. I hear Angela lock the front door and follow them into the condo.

"Almost killed myself slipping on that frickin' hill. Just a mild ankle sprain, I hope. I had a good look at what was happening and then when I saw them approach you with the knife, I knew I had to act." That's the one on the left. His voice is trailing away from me so he must have turned to talk to Angela. The one on the right is inches away from me now.

"How'd you get the drop on Brew? Did we get a direct hit? Those rubber bullets are a bitch. I tried to aim high since you were on the couch, but they don't fly true like normal rounds. Nailed the Asian dude." The agent right beside me taps on his rifle and turns towards Angela as he chuckles.

It's time.

The twine around my wrists snaps easily. Before Lead Foot knows what's happening, I'm on him—but I've misjudged him. I'm going to call this one Johnson. He's overweight, all right, but there's quite a bit of muscle. He's built like a football player. The element of surprise has given me a slight advantage. I grab him by the hips and kick him hard in the back of his knee. As it buckles, I wrap my arm around his neck in a sleeper hold.

Holley's face is rife with shock. He lifts his semiautomatic. I don't know if the bullets in his chamber are still rubber, and this is no time for roulette.

But it doesn't matter.

Angela's kick to Holley's injured ankle sends his bullets spraying towards the ceiling. Because his hands are on his weapon, he doesn't have time to break his fall. She's already on top of him, flipping him onto his back with one hand as the other lands a blow to his nose, slamming his head violently into the foyer linoleum.

I'm so distracted by her efficiency that I forget about Johnson. Maybe he wanted me to forget him. For a moment he stops struggling and his body goes limp, and for a split second I think I've knocked him out. But in an instant, he grabs his rifle and rams the butt into my ribcage. The searing pain turns my vision white and I nearly let go. Nearly. The stakes are too high. That was his only chance. Had I let up at all, he might have turned the tables, but that last effort spends him. Seconds later, he passes out. I hold him an extra ten seconds to be sure.

During that time, Angela puts the finishing touches on Holley, clearly concussed after having his head bounced like a basketball on linoleum. A swift kick to the face and he's out. She disarms him and looks in the magazine clip.

"Live rounds. That was close." She glances at Holley and adds, "Never liked him anyway. Creeper."

Her plan had worked. I'm in the process of lowering Johnson to the ground when I hear the sound of crunching glass behind me. It only takes a glance at Angela's horrified face to spur me into action. I release Johnson's hulking frame. The assault rifle strapped around his neck falls with him. Before it hits the ground, I kick my foot upwards, launching rifle and strap into the air and off of the slumping Johnson. I catch the weapon midair and spin to my right, spotting an armed agent in black thirty-three feet away and advancing through the shattered patio door. I light him up, the recoil of the gun blistering my already aching right flank. The agent drops his weapon as he falls back, taking several bullets to the upper torso. He groans on the ground, clutching his battered body.

I look back at Angela, whose mouth hangs open. She's still holding the magazine. I'm not sure if she is more surprised at my skills or that there was a third agent.

"He . . . he must be one of the new interns. Holley didn't mention that when I texted him, I swear. Jesus, that was close."

"Any other surprises, Angela?" I ask, casually resting the rifle on my shoulder, my finger still on the trigger.

"I think I should be asking you that question . . ."

Chapter 16

10:35 A.M.

Angela and I cuff the three agents' hands behind their backs, attached to each other, with their own equipment. I attend to Chang, who has crawled to the piano bench and is trying to pull himself to a stand.

"Take it easy, friend. That could have been a lot worse."

He pats me on the shoulder as I help him to his feet. "Benjamin, these are just flesh wounds. Don't worry about me. You need to get out of here."

"Chang, you need medical attention. Let me hel—"

"Brew, he's right," Angela interjects. "We gotta go. Those guys don't radio in, there will be backup here in no time." She zips up her jacket and heads to the door.

"No, not *we*. Angela, take Chang somewhere safe. Local hospital, nearby relative. I'll take the car the Gs left and head home. I need to make sure my family is ok. Hopefully, I'll have a plan by the time I get there."

"Won't they be waiting at home for you? Don't you think we should stay together?"

"Nobody knows about your involvement yet except for the people in this room. Place a call to the agency and set them on a cold trail. Tell them I got spooked and bolted for DC, that the tactical team is on my trail." I check the time on my phone.

"Ok, that could work. At least it will buy you a little time. Meet up at your place in thirty minutes?"

"Perfect. And Angela ... thanks," I say, looking directly into her eyes. "Couldn't have done it without you."

She nods. "We're in the same boat now. We need to make this right. Not just for the two of us. But for every soldier, agent out there that's got one of these chips."

We share a quick hug before I turn to Jang-Ho. "Chang, you're in good hands. Stay safe, and I hope we can have a beer when this is all over, talk things through, mend some fences. And if you don't mind, I'll take a rain check on the earlobectomy."

Chang looks up at me, his blood-smeared face brightening for a moment. "Ugh, chip doesn't get rid of bad joke-telling? Yet another glitch you'll have to fix in version 2.1."

Chapter 17

11:55 A.M.

I'm in a black government sedan and about five minutes from my house. I ditched the SIM card in my phone so I can't be traced—Angela gave me that tip. I see seven missed calls from Amy. I'm praying everything is ok. I listen to the most recent voicemail and it sounds like she's home and safe and worried about me. That message was eight minutes ago. I've been a bit preoccupied.

I'm trying to think through how I'm going to explain to her what's going on with me. How do I tell her I've lost every memory I've ever had of knowing her? How do I tell her it's because of a microchip I helped create?

And then how do I fix this mess?

I pull into the driveway and rest my forehead against the steering wheel. I'm not worried about the agency right now. The street is clear. I wasn't followed. Hopefully Angela's diversion is working, for now. I do what feels natural as I sit there in the quiet car: I pray. I may have lost my memories, but I haven't forgotten my faith.

I ask God for guidance. I thank him for life, a beautiful wife, beautiful kids. I thank him for all the goodness I perceive in my life, even the stuff I don't remember. But I also ask his forgiveness. I know I've played a role in this mess. I beg him for a chance to make things right, for the good of my family, for the good of the soldiers and agents who deserve better. Lastly, I ask him for strength. I end my prayer awkwardly but immediately feel better. Not a surge of confidence, but a sense of peace. A sense that everything is going to be ok.

I enter the house through the garage. Amy is waiting for me in the kitchen. She jumps into my arms and squeezes me tight. I grimace a little from the pain in my side.

"Honey, I'm so sorry I've been absent today. I've had the strangest day." I hold her at arms' length and look deeply into her eyes. "I don't even know where to begin."

She places a finger over my lips and shushes me. "Sit down, let me get you something to drink."

The lyrical undulation of her voice is soothing, but underneath it I sense some anxiety. Wait ... am I kidding myself? I've known "my wife" for all of thirty minutes. It's hard to trust instincts without having the memories that forged them. I take a seat at the round table on the other side of the kitchen bar. It feels great to stretch out my aching legs.

I close my eyes for a few precious seconds, listening to Amy moving mechanically around in the kitchen. The sound of the fridge's ice dispenser doesn't even jar me, I'm so tired.

I hear her steps approaching and I open my eyes. She holds an ice-filled glass of soda in one hand and a can of Dr. Pepper in the other. Dr. Pepper has been my favorite drink . . . since I was in high school . . . and I was in high school last night. I guess some things don't change.

I take the glass from her hands and touch her forearm lightly in appreciation. Then I ask her the first question that comes to mind. "Did you notice I was a little . . . off . . . this morning?"

"I mean, you are forty today, ha ha," she nervously chuckles. She spins on a dime and walks quickly back towards the kitchen counter.

I echo her chuckle. Hmm . . . she's not acting quite right, but . . . maybe it's just me. How do I know how she's supposed to act? This morning I didn't even know her name. I stare into the glass of Dr. Pepper, realizing I haven't had anything to eat or drink all day. Then it dawns on me that Amy might be nervous because I look fairly disheveled. I haven't really had time to clean myself up since my various, uh, altercations. So why hasn't she said anything about my appearance?

"Amy, I can explain the cuts and blood. But before I say anything else, just know that I love you. I really do." I'm not sure why I say those words. It's weird, because deep down, I really do feel love for her, and I can't explain it. My brain can't pull up a single memory of her before today, but there's this gnawing feeling in my gut that says I love this woman.

She turns to face me, her hands behind her back. She looks beautiful. Her dolphin-blue eyes are full of . . . fear. While I wait for her to say something, anything, I take a long swig of the Dr. Pepper. Real long. I down all of it, thirstier than I realized. I put the glass down. The burn of the soda lingers in my throat and chest, but there's an aftertaste that reminds me of . . . of . . .

I look back at Amy. She takes a step towards me and pauses. *Maybe I said the wrong thing.* And then she takes another tentative step, and then another, hands still behind her back. She seems to be shaking. I splay out my arms invitingly when she's a few steps away.

"Sweetie, are you ok? You look pale." And then I begin to feel strangely woozy. My outstretched arms become incredibly heavy, as if someone attached thirty-pound dumbbells to my wrists. The room is starting to spin. I now see one, two, three Amys. I clumsily reach out to grab one of them and get a handful of air, losing my balance and tumbling to the floor. Rolling onto my back now, I shake my head to clear the cobwebs, but they thicken instead, and I'm looking at the world through smudged glass lenses. The trio of fuzzy Amys now stands directly over me, and I weakly lift my right arm in expectation of a helping hand to get back into my chair. Amy brings her hands in front of her.

She is holding a large serrated kitchen knife.

Shit. *Trust no one* . . . Chang's words echo in a distant part of my foggy brain.

With all of my remaining energy, I flip myself onto my stomach and attempt to crawl away, but my legs won't move. Behind me, I hear Amy saying, "Ben, I'm so sorry, I'm so sorry."

And then the room goes black.

Chapter 18

12:12 P.M.

I'm regaining consciousness. My thoughts are coming into focus before my eyes, and the first thing that pops into my head: *My wife . . . she . . . she drugged me. She's working with the agency?*

But at least I'm alive—she didn't kill me with the knife she was holding. And in other good news, my head is feeling a bit better. The buzzing has stopped. I am suddenly aware of a sticky substance on the back of my head. I reach up to feel what it is, perhaps too quickly. *Owww . . .* The right side of my ribcage is killing me. Oh yeah, I got jabbed in the chest with a rifle earlier. When I bring my hand back to my face, I'm surprised to see what can only be . . . my own blood.

I'm lying in a pool of my own blood.

My senses are attuned to what sounds like sobbing coming from another room. It's getting closer. It's Amy. She's sobbing the same way she did when we had to take Ana in for surgery to remove an infected lymph node from her neck. When I discovered the node, I was terrified it was cancer but did not tell Amy. It was the first time one of our children was really sick. It scared the bejeebers out of both of us—even me, the physician. It's way different when it's your own child. In the end, Ana was fine. But I'll never forget how my wife cried that day.

She rounds the corner and sees me awake. Keeping her distance, she covers her mouth with her hand as I sit up. Her eyes widen. She doesn't look menacing, but I look for a weapon anyway. Maybe she wasn't holding a knife when she approached me before; I couldn't see all that well. But there's no doubt she drugged me. I guess I hit my head really hard when I fell out of my chair.

"It's ok, sweetie, I'm fine." My voice sounds strained and I realize she is probably not reassured.

"Are you . . . are you back?"

I'm a little confused. She points at my face.

"What? The blood?" I ask.

"No, your ear."

I reach up to my left ear. The bottom half has been sheared off.

And suddenly, it's all coming back.

I am back.

Chapter 19

12:17 P.M.

It's obvious now. How else could I have remembered the story of Ana's infected lymph node? There are still a few cobwebs, but I feel like myself again. It's almost like bumping into an old friend I haven't seen for years, except the old friend is . . . me.

"Yes, Ames," I respond, confident. "I'm back."

I can see relief wash over her as she runs over to help me to my feet. We hug for what feels like hours, my gut and my brain finally connecting, that feeling of love I felt for her earlier fully complete. As I hold her in my arms, I indulge in a quick skip down memory lane, enjoying the memories of our first meeting at Harvard, our courtship and marriage, having kids. I feel alive again! We release each other and she guides me to a chair and sits on my lap. I spend four minutes recapping my day. She spends two minutes recapping hers. She admits to noticing I was acting a little strange this morning. Not going for my morning workout. Not taking Kobi to daycare. That was especially notable, as that ritual is some of my favorite daddy time of the week. I made the girls one gigantic plate of scrambled eggs. That's not like me. I'm more of a short-order chef—my kids mock me for calling myself the Gordon Ramsay of breakfast. Ana and Gabri prefer their eggs over medium, while Kobi likes scrambled with cheese.

"You knew that early in the day? Why didn't you say something?" But as soon as I ask those questions, I have questions for myself. What should she have said? It's not like she knew I had lost my memory. Could she have stopped anything that's happened so far today?

And from the way I'm lost in my thoughts, Amy can probably tell that she doesn't need to answer my ridiculous questions. She continues to recap her day.

"After you left the house and I dropped Kobi off at daycare, I checked my voicemail and saw a message from you from 11:25 last night. You must have called my phone and left a message after I'd fallen asleep," she says, making a quick glance at her phone on the table. "You know I sleep like a rock, so you must have guessed I wouldn't check my messages until morning. But you also know I'm terrible at finding my phone. Half the time I don't even plug it in before going to bed. Let's be honest; I'm way less addicted to technology than you," she chuckles. "That being said, it was smart of you to charge it for me and leave it on my nightstand."

She winks at me and reaches for her phone. She pushes a few buttons and within seconds we are listening to my deep voice, rushed and anxious:

"Amy, there's no time to explain. I think I have a memory chip implanted in my ear that I fear the government is going to use to erase my memory. I know it sounds strange. Crazy, actually. But I need you to believe me. If I'm acting strange tomorrow in any way—asking questions that I should know, maybe not doing my usual daddy things—my memory has been erased and I'm faking being fine, because I'm probably scared. I need you to do something really important. It's the hardest thing I've ever asked you to do . . . I need you to cut off the bottom of my ear. Not sure which one. But hey, you have a 50/50 chance of getting it right. Maybe flip a coin? <nervous laugh> I've drawn you a picture and placed it in your dresser drawer, complete with directions on how to cut it off. You're going to have to drug me. Give me a glass of orange juice with this powdered drug mixed in well—also in your dresser drawer. You have to trust me on this. The safety of our family, our kids—depends on your actions. I know you can do it, Ames. Try to do it before I leave the house in the morning. If I'm away when you get this, call me and make up an emergency to get me home. But as soon as you see me, you've got to do it. By the time you get this it may already be too late. I love you. I'm praying for God to give you strength. Mwah." End of message.

Amy didn't disappoint.

After following my instructions to the best of her ability (we were out of orange juice, and she was fortunate that Dr. Pepper masked the drug's taste reasonably well), she ran to the bathroom to throw up her turkey-bacon ranch wrap. She made multiple trips apparently, between retching and coming out to check on me to make sure I was still breathing.

Amy finishes telling me all this as I keep pressure on my ear to stop the bleeding. She has a suture kit on the table as well as a tiny Ziploc bag full of . . . bloody ice?

"I thought you might . . . maybe once the chip is removed you can have it sewn back on?"

She is adorable. I picked a keeper. How many women will drug you, cut off part of your ear based on an insane voicemail, and then put your earlobe on ice for safekeeping? I'm just glad she picked the correct ear. I didn't really give her instructions on what to do if she picked the wrong one. Things might have gotten ugly, especially if I hadn't spoken to Chang yet and woke up with no idea what was going on.

I put my arms around Amy and hold her tight. I feel terrible for the trauma I've put her through. Shoot, I should feel bad for the trauma she's put me through, even though I asked for it. I suppress a giggle and let her out of my grasp, checking the paper towel that's sticking to my left ear and now my fingers. The bleeding has stopped. I grab the suture kit and walk into the bathroom. Within a few minutes, I've stitched the gaping wound in my ear.

Amy stands at the door. I look at her troubled face in the mirror.

"So what next? I'm scared, Ben. Really scared," she says, her voice trembling, her arms crossed against her chest. "Who are you? Why did the government put a chip in your ear? Is this why you've been acting weird for the last . . . last year?"

I feel my head starting to clear. It's understandable she has a lot of questions. *Weird for the last year.* That's pretty damning. I'm just happy remembering that yesterday I was thirty-nine years old. Except . . . I can't seem to remember everything from yesterday. Just bits and pieces. Not enough to really be able to answer her last two questions, so I'll start with her first. It's the most important one to her anyway. Involving her in this has created a host of other troubling questions, no doubt.

"To be honest, Ames? The government chip stuff, my behavior over the last year? Those questions are tough to answer with my brain still so . . . foggy. The question as to who I am? That's crystal clear. You know who I am. I'm still your Benjamin. But what I do for a living? Let me give you the two-minute version."

It takes me twice that long to explain my work for the agency. Telling my best friend I've kept secrets because information is classified or vital to national security doesn't really make her feel any better; I can tell by the look on her face. I feel like a liar. I'd thought this day would come, but we'd be old lovers, sitting on the porch swing sipping iced tea, and then in subtle fashion, I'd drop the whole special-ops training, president's-daughter bit. This is a tad sooner than expected, and I'm not prepared.

We're still standing in the bathroom when I finish my explanation.

"So my husband is a doctor AND an agent for the government . . . ok. What now?"

That was not the response I expected . . . but it's the response I should have expected. I married an intelligent woman. She's grounded. She knows there's no time for the wounded, left-in-the-dark spouse routine. My life, her life, the kids' lives—the life we built together—is at serious risk. She needs Benjamin the butt-kicking government agent/doctor right now, not Benjamin the duplicitous, repentant husband. She certainly doesn't need an eighteen-year-old boy trapped in a forty-year-old's body. And with my memory back, I can finally answer that eighteen-year-old boy's question definitively: *No, I'm not a ninja.* Dang it.

"What now?" I echo back to her. "I don't have a plan yet, Ames. I need a minute."

But I don't know if another minute is really going to make a difference. My memory is back. Mostly. I'm having trouble differentiating what Chang told me yesterday in our phone call and what actually happened yesterday. I'm having trouble remembering that I met with the director at all. Sure, everything else Chang and I talked about feels accessible: my time in his lab at Harvard, my additional work in med school and residency, my time at the wounded-warrior clinic with the second-gen chip.

Wait. That's it. That was two years ago. I remember an encounter I had with the director about putting that chip into soldiers without their consent:

I am standing in the director's office on the thirtieth floor looking out over the sprawling city. I can't look him in the eye. He sits at his desk poring over the data I emailed him earlier in the day.

"But you've shown that we can erase memory, Ben. Selectively. This can and will work for PTSD." He is giddy as he feverishly clicks his mouse. I don't share his enthusiasm.

"WE? WE . . . my research partners and I . . . WE don't have the clearance to do this. I'm not even sure it's ethical. We've only shown it in mice, for crying out loud. We need years of human testing bef—"

"Of course, of course," he interrupts me. "But you've already had some success in your human studies of Alzheimer's patients. So you'd be ok with it if we, I mean, I . . . gave soldiers a choice?"

His eyes look crazed. I'm worried. "I don't know. It just seems like there's so much potential for abuse. And what if the deployment was a time of growth? And what if that stress is important? I've been doing a lot of reading on post-traumatic growth recently. Powerful stuff. We shouldn't be messing with people's brains like this. Preserving memory in Alzheimer's and neurodegenerative brain disorders is one thing. Deleting memories? This is something entirely different."

I wish my memory of what immediately followed this conversation was fuzzy, but it's not. I know exactly what I did, what I agreed to that very next day. Sure, some of the memories of the director and me in the months that followed are patchy. It's like after that conversation with the director, he and I didn't talk about it anymore. Though I distinctly remember seeing soldiers in the wounded-warrior clinic; in my mind's eye, I can see them happy, doing well in recovery. Thanking me. Not complaining of significant PTSD.

So there's no question in my mind that we implanted chips into soldiers . . . probably without their consent. And now my mind leads me to the issue at hand . . . yes . . . Carrie, the president's daughter. Chang said I was concerned about her behavior, and that she might have a chip. That would be an even grosser misuse of the technology than implanting the chip involuntarily in soldiers. I'm searching my thoughts to figure out how or when Carrie got one. Blank.

"Ben? You still there?"

I've been staring at myself in the mirror this whole time when Amy's voice brings me back to earth.

"Yeah . . . I . . . I think I know what I need to do," I respond.

"I'm glad to hear th—"

The sound of the back door creaking open, followed by the crescendo of deliberate footsteps approaching the kitchen, snaps me to attention. I pull Amy into the bathroom and turn off the lights, my left hand forming a snug seal over her mouth. I grab the scissors from the suturing kit and hold them like a weapon—ready for whatever comes around the corner.

Sigh.

I relax my grip and let Amy go, stepping out of the shadows and into the lamp-lit hallway.

It's Angela.

"Hey, I let myself in. You know there's a cleanup needed on aisle two over there . . . wowsers . . . that's quite a bit of blood. You forgot your tampon, Brew? What happened?"

She looks at my face, then my ear, and gasps. "Oh. That's hardcore. You did that yourself?"

"No. Amy did it. Amy, this is Angela, my, uh, partner." I awkwardly point across my body in Angela's general direction without making eye contact with either woman. "Angela, this is Amy, my wife. Sorry to introduce the two of you under these circumstances."

"Was there ever going to be a good time, Ben?" I brace for the worst, given the tone of Amy's voice. "What are you and Angela going to do?"

I sneak a look over at Amy, who exudes determination. She has a knack for being direct— probably from her experience starting up and running her own businesses. She deserves a direct answer.

"Amy, I've got to go back in," I say, turning to face her. "To the agency. When I met with the director, I found out he had tagged a civilian. The details are fuzzy in my mind, but basically he has been erasing this civilian's memory, selectively. She's just a college kid. She has no idea."

"That's what this is all about? Just one teenager?"

"She's not just any teenager," I chide. "And no, it's not just about her. I know there's more. My gut tells me there's more. I just can't put a finger on it."

Angela puffs her cheeks then forcefully blows out through pursed lips. "You're going to the agency to talk with the director again? In case you've forgotten, that didn't work out too well the first time."

Forgotten? I doubt her word choice is accidental. "No more talking. I'm going to the agency to turn off that college kid's chip. And every chip that's been implanted in our soldiers and agents over the last few years. Whatever the director is up to ends today."

Chapter 20

12:37 P.M.

I've changed into fresh clothes— white shirt, black tie, standard drab agency dress—and for some dumb reason, all I'm worried about is my Van Gogh ear bleeding onto this Hugo Boss, French cuff cotton dress shirt Amy bought me last Christmas. Angela checks the magazine of the Beretta 9mm she took off the rookie agent at Chang's condo. "Well, we better get moving," she says, holstering the gun under her jacket. "Our three disabled agents would have missed their check-in by now. It won't be long till they track us down. By the way, Chang is safe at a hotel in Virginia Beach. Paid for in cash so he should be untraceable."

I nod approvingly, then cock my head and ask, "So I guess there's no convincing you to sit this one out?"

Angela looks at me quizzically. "Umm . . . when I tried to drug you, took out three agents, then found out about a plot to control me by erasing my memories? Nope, I think I'm in."

Angela nervously rubs her ear. I get it. Fearing that at any moment, someone could flip a switch and erase parts of your past, good or bad, without consent? Pretty troubling. My mind wanders to the birth of Kobi, the moment her head got briefly stuck in the birth canal, my anxiety (and hiding those anxious feelings from Amy as she pushed), the moment Kobi got unstuck, followed by her first cry and my tears of joy for a third time during the birth of a child. That memory had been suppressed twenty minutes ago—gone, for all I know. What if I had lost that memory, never again able to retrieve it? The thought stokes my anger. I ball my hands into tight fists.

My gaze falls on Amy, who sits at the dining table quietly cradling a cup of coffee like a newborn baby's head, and I force myself to relax. The mother of my children hasn't said a word for the last five minutes. She is watching my every move, though. She's probably never seen me with a holster or a gun. In my regular life, I hate guns. Heck, I hate them in my secret life, too, but I've learned to treat them as tools . . . like a scalpel in the hands of a surgeon. A good surgeon will avoid surgery if possible, and I only use my gun to deter or eliminate extreme threats, and for nothing more. There are other less lethal tools at my disposal.

"Have you killed anybody?"

I was waiting for that question. Kinda nice to know if the person sleeping next to you every night has blood on their hands. I answer honestly. "Yes, but not recently. And only when my life, or someone else's, depended on it."

Amy doesn't say anything. She doesn't have to. Problem is, I don't know what to say right now. There's not enough time to say everything I need to say.

"Amy, I'm sor—"

"Shhhh. Ben, I love you. Do what you need to do to keep me and the girls safe. You always have. You need to go ... before I ask you one hundred more questions."

She flashes me that toothy smile that has sustained me for the last two decades. A peace fills my soul. I walk towards her chair and embrace her, holding her head against my abdomen and stroking her blond locks. I kiss the top of her head tenderly.

"Ben, there's one more thing."

She pulls out a book that's been sitting in her lap. I recognize it immediately. It's a diary she gave me eight years ago for our tenth anniversary. I'm not big into journaling. I tried using it when she first got it for me, but I can't remember using it over the last several years. The next thing she says makes me ill.

"You once told me that if you ever started acting weird, I should feel free to read your diary. That no thoughts should be kept secret from me. That sounds funny in the moment. But I have been checking your diary from time to time over the past year. It's really strange. There are dated entries ... but no text. Just numbers." She opens to the most recent entry and shows me.

Nov 1, 2020. 53325480

I'm confused. What the hell does this mean? Coordinates? Serial numbers? For what? There are dozen of dates with entries consisting only of eight-digit numbers. I take the diary and kiss Amy's head again, my mind racing.

Yet another puzzle to solve. And I'm pissed off because my memory is back and I can't remember how to solve a puzzle I created! It'll come to me. If it's important to what's happening today, it'll come to me.

Chapter 21

14:10 P.M.

It feels good to be moving again. Even if we're moving towards an objective that, frankly, could end in disaster. The simple act of looking out of my window makes me appreciate having my memories back. The fact that I recognize the buildings I'm driving by is incredibly comforting. A few hours ago, I felt like a foreigner in a strange land, like a freshman on his first day of high school. Now I'm a citizen with a purpose. I'm a husband, a father, a wannabe good guy. We're only five minutes away from HQ now. Angela nervously plays with her left ear.

"Do you even know where you're going?" she asks me. "Especially since you still seem a little fuzzy?"

That's the thing. I'm not fuzzy. I know how to access the computer that controls the microchips. It's on Level -1. I know the room because I helped the engineers create it. But I only have faint memories of using the mainframe. The worst part about having my memory back? I'm now aware of my role in this mess. I'm not ready to tell Angela that *I* spearheaded the effort to put the microchips in soldiers.

I keep going back to why we created the mainframe room in the first place: to help the soldiers who voluntarily signed up to receive the chip. At their request, we could erase the most traumatic parts of their deployment, if they provided us a specific date and time. At least that's what I thought we told them. Given my own situation, I now know this was not the case for everyone.

"Can you explain again how this chip works?" Angela blurts out. Her earlobes have developed a deep red hue from being rubbed raw over the past hour. "I know we don't have all day, but maybe I'll cut my own ear off by day's end if I know what you know."

I give her the high-school-graduate version—the MD/PhD version would take days to explain. The science behind the chip goes back centuries. Acupuncture. Specifically, auricular acupuncture, or AA. The main tenet of AA is that the entire body is mapped to the ear, an aural homunculus, much like the homunculus on the cortex of the brain. Stick a needle into the cortical part of the brain that represents the hand, and a finger moves. Poke the part that represents the lower spine, and the back muscles tense up. For centuries, AA was widely used for physical ailments. More recently it has been used to address mental-health disorders like anxiety and depression. How? By targeting parts of the aural homunculus that represent parts of the brain that are tied to emotion and memory. The hippocampus. The amygdala. Jang-Ho Chang had learned acupuncture from his grandmother—he stumbled upon the idea when thinking back to how she treated his anxiety in middle school, shunning doctors who had tried to place him on what she called "mind-altering drugs." Chang postulated that if needles implanted superficially into the hippocampal region of the ear could ease formation of anxious memories, maybe something more permanent, like a chip, could be used to control memory.

The first generation was initially just like my Fisher-Price tape recorder. Upon activation, the chip recorded memories. Well, the chip itself wasn't recording memories. The brain, specifically the hippocampus, was doing all of the hard work. The chip, placed in the hippocampal region of the ear's homunculus, stimulated the brain's hippocampus to basically record in overdrive. New memories created from the moment the chip was activated were consolidated *stronger*. Imagine saving a file to your laptop's hard drive, then backing it up on a writable CD/DVD, as well as storing it in a physical digital data hub in your closet, as well as in the cloud. This is essentially what the microchip stimulated the brain to do: store new memories in multiple ways to ensure better preservation. And old memories prior to the chip being placed? Early results from our mice experiments suggested that those old memories remained strong and were less susceptible to loss than they'd been before.

"But how did you find mice with memory issues? Did you put up flyers in Harvard Square soliciting rats who got lost frequently on the subway?"

Ha ha. People often use humor to hide their fear. I certainly do, but I'm waaay funnier. Angela is eager to hear more, and to calm her fears, I laugh at her attempt at humor and upgrade her explanation to the postgraduate level.

"Chang and I were working with a transgenic mouse model designed with genes implicated in the development of Alzheimer's disease." A glance over at Angela's owl-wide eyes forces a loud snicker from the depths of my nose.

"Ok, ok, so in layman's terms, we bred mice with Alzheimer's disease who, as they grew older, exhibited many of the same symptoms humans with Alzheimer's exhibit. These mice forgot mazes and other memory-based activities we had taught them *before* they developed Alzheimer's symptoms. But those mice with chips implanted early on during symptom development? Much better outcomes in terms of memory preservation and the ability to form new memories.

"Like all amazing scientific discoveries, it was an accident that gave us a window onto the chip's other capabilities. Our in-house tech genius was working late one night making modifications to the chip on his PC. He thought he was modifying the coding of in vitro microchips, chips still sitting in packaging on the lab benches. But he was actually modifying *in vivo* chips—chips in live mice. What we discovered was that live mice that had just shown proficiency in a specific maze completely lost the ability to do that maze with one simple modification to the code. Once we were able to replicate the results, it was clear we had something groundbreaking on our hands, and that the memory of learning the maze wasn't completely gone—just fuzzed out. The memory loss was completely reversible. But our real mistake—my real mistake—was sharing this information with the government."

Angela shifts uncomfortably in her seat, the tips of her fingers still nibbling at her ears. I dread continuing because I know she's not going to like this next part.

I have always had a soft spot in my heart for the military. Hard not to, given my history . . . I immediately knew that our chip could do veterans some good. War is ugly and leaves scars. I really thought this chip, this second-generation chip that could selectively wipe memories, was the answer. But I got in too deep. When I realized the potential danger, I tried to shut down the project. Partially. I was assured by the director and the military brass that getting chipped was optional for deploying soldiers. Until it wasn't.

How could I have let this happen?

I realize this last bit of dialogue has been completely internal, as if I'm trying to defend myself in the courtroom of my own twisted brain. Angela nods, not because any words have come out of my mouth for the last several seconds, but because she's smart enough to guess what I've done.

"So, first soldiers, then agents, then civilians?"

My mouth is dry. "To be honest, I don't know how the president's daughter came into play, but somewhere along the way, Carrie got a chip. And someone has been systematically erasing her memories. For the life of me I don't know why—for her own protection, I'm sure."

"That's funny, I thought protecting Carrie was my job," Angela interjects.

I don't know how to respond to that other than continuing. "These memory wipes are getting dangerous and must stop. Carrie's beginning to second-guess whether she's taken her antiepileptic meds or not. That's a problem. Miss too many doses and she could fall into status epilepticus— a continuous seizure that's hard to break. Deadly. Not good."

"None of that gave me the warm fuzzies, Brew. But here we are." I turn onto Armistead Avenue. The gate up ahead is flanked by guards carrying AR-47s.

"So what's your brilliant plan for getting us in?"

I allow myself the tiniest of smiles. "That's just it, Ang. We're just going to drive up, park, and walk right in. Just like old times."

Chapter 22

1415

And so far, my plan is working. We drive right in. Nobody questions my badge at the gate. The guards even smile and greet me, as usual. I have been banking on the assumption that the director does NOT want my situation to be a big deal. He doesn't want the whole agency knowing about it. This is all about information containment. What I don't know is how long he is going to let me play out this charade. My estimation is that I have nine minutes from the moment my badge is registered at the gate. Nine minutes. Angela doesn't like the fact that I'll save time by having her drop me at the door. I tell her I'll catch up with her later, but I have every intention of ditching her. I need to face the director alone.

I'm nervous as I enter through the main doors. Nothing seems amiss. No one appears to be paying any special attention to me, not even the armed guards in the lobby. The afternoon sun shines brightly through the arched glass roof of the entryway, and in my nervousness I find myself staring at my shadow as I walk towards the weapons locker. I check my gun in before walking through the metal detectors, my heart thumping 110 beats per minute. Once I'm through, I relax, but only slightly. I scan the room and seconds later bump into Jason Dunlap from International Finance. He leads me through an elaborate cool-kids handshake that ends with him snapping his fingers. I'm pretty sure he's still watching reruns of *The Fresh Prince of Bel-Air*. I'm not sure who I hate more: him for making me do the handshake or myself for playing along. Jason reminds me we have a pickup basketball game in three days. I tell him I'll be there to do my best Kobe Bryant impersonation and he chuckles and punches me in the arm and feigns boxing me out. He looks to ask about my ear and I preempt him by pointing at the bandage and saying "hairy-ear shaving accident." I mimic dribbling a basketball and lean my shoulder into his chest. He chuckles again as we part ways.

That took thirty-six seconds too long.

As I hurry towards the elevators, I try to anticipate the director's next moves. I know he doesn't want to announce that one of his best agents has gone rogue. He's eager to contain this. It's why he erased my memory. There's something I know that no one else should know. And it seems kind of dumb to point out the obvious—people with high security clearance know classified stuff that other people shouldn't know. But whatever is jostling around in my head like a puppy in a box under a Christmas tree, must be big. Yeah, the president's daughter has a chip, and that's a big freaking deal—but that can't be it. There must be more to it.

I pick an empty elevator to give myself time to get ready. I'm unarmed; agency rules. Other than the security guards, no one carries a gun in HQ. But there are other weapons, and though I'm not expecting resistance, I am prepared. I swipe my badge over the keypad and press -1. The elevator begins its silent descent. A full twenty seconds later, it comes to a halt. I close my eyes and take a deep breath. The doors open.

A tear-gas grenade rolls into the elevator and explodes, filling the car with smoke. Three gas-mask-wearing Gs approach cautiously with guns raised. There's violent coughing as the smoke clears. They enter the elevator and freeze. There are two people on their hands and knees rubbing their eyes with the backs of their hands. The Gs drag them out and look at their bleary faces. I am not one of them.

Chapter 23

1423

Level -1 isn't some super-secret level of the agency, but it is the first of the basement levels. It's not like Level -2 or -3. Interrogations happen on those levels, so I'm told; some questionably legal stuff. Stuff the ACLU would have a field day over. Lots of folks have access to Level -1, though, which makes it a great place to hide things you don't want people to view as suspicious.

I am not in the smoked-filled elevator because I am two steps ahead of the director. The extra thirty-six seconds I spent with Jason Dunlap weren't wasted. I yanked that chump's ID badge when we were choreographing basketball moves. I knew it wouldn't take him long to notice, so I made my move to the elevators quickly.

There are three elevators in the Mason Foyer. They are each separated by about eight feet. One minute ago, I picked the farthest one to the left. I got on with two suit-wearing, baby-faced employees (probably interns, given the lack of facial hair and confidence), the eager type looking to impress the higher-ups in Jason Dunlap's finance subdivision. I felt sorry (ok, not that sorry) for what I suspected was about to happen to them. On the elevator, I swiped my badge and pushed -1. As the door closed, I stuck my hand out, jarring it open. I apologized under my breath and slipped off the elevator. But according to someone's computer in a security room on the east wing of the first floor, Benjamin Brew is on Elevator 1.

I sprint to the elevator on the opposite end and push the button. When I get on Elevator 3, I instruct the three people waiting with me to take the next elevator. They don't question me. I used Dunlap's ID to swipe myself into Level -1. I'm guessing I'll arrive about sixteen seconds after the car I just left.

My tImtiming is near perfect. As I step off my elevator, the smoke is already clearing. I am now standing directly behind the third agent. The other two (I'm assuming at least two) must be in the elevator trying to identify which one of the two suffering schleps is me.

I am holding my telescoping baton in my right hand. The director only sent three agents to subdue me. *Tsk, tsk.*

Agent #3 doesn't know what hit him when I put him in a sleeper hold and drag him away from the elevator. He's out in seconds. The other two are dragging out the groaning employees. I'm on them in a flash, clipping the one on the left in the back of the knee with the heel of my boot, then dealing a swift blow to the back of his neck with my baton. His head bounces off the ground, which alerts the other agent, who lets go of the sports coat he is holding to reach for his weapon. I strike his wrist and hear a crunch. He withdraws in pain but doesn't have time to dwell on his broken radius before I swiftly kick the inner aspect of his left knee, severely spraining his lateral collateral ligament and dropping him to the ground. Two blows to his head and he's out. I rip the gas mask off of his face.

My baton securely back in my lower pant-leg pocket, I walk away from the carnage towards Room - 1M, my footsteps making no sound on the white tile floor. The hall is decorated with photographs and paintings capturing over sixty years of agency history, much like the other floors, and is dimly lit. I've always thought of it as mood lighting for the defenders of freedom. Helps everyone takes their job more seriously than they already do. At the end of the long hallway, I take a left. I have no idea what's to the right because I've never gone that way. My feet are virtually on autopilot at this point. Eighteen more steps until I'm there.

I biometrically swipe myself into the room. It's quiet. The lights are already on. Three steps in and the only direction to go is left, after which a short hallway opens onto a large, unfurnished office. I pause before making the turn, getting an overwhelming feeling of déjà vu, so much so I'm sick to my stomach. The mainframe computer, the computer that controls all the chips, is only seconds away. As I slowly make the turn, a solitary figure stands at the keyboard, back to me.

"Hello, Benjamin." This comes off as more of an acknowledgment of my presence than a greeting. "I should have sent more men." He turns to me. The smug look on his face is nauseating. This isn't the first time in the last forty years I've wanted to strike him, but the thought has occurred with increasing regularity over the last few years.

"Hello, Dad."

Chapter 24

1424

"I didn't want to have to do it. You forced my hand," he says, shrugging, hands clasped at his waist.

"So you wiped twenty-two years of my memory? Ok, Dad, that seems fair." I struggle not to raise my voice. In this chess match, I can't show weakness. Emotion is weakness. "Doesn't seem like you really thought this through. What did you think was going to happen? That I'd be ok with feeling like an eighteen-year-old trapped in a forty-year-old's body? Or that I wouldn't be smart enough to anticipate your next move, as heartless as it was?" *Pawn to d4. His move.*

My father's voice drones—he knows the game. It's as if he's talking to me about my Fisher-Price tape. "It's a matter of national security. You should understand that. When I selected you for this role as doctor to the president's teenage daughter, you understood the risks." He shuffles to his left. *Knight to f6. Back at me.*

"Was one of those risks that my own father would fry my memory?" I ask sarcastically. I've taken a few steps forward until I'm six feet away from him. *Pawn to c4.*

"After the things you said yesterday, I . . . I had no choice." *Pawn to e5.*

My dad probably fails to see the irony of his words. *No choice.* But I'm not going to let him blame this on me, so I press forward. "What the hell did I say yesterday? Even after removing the stupid chip, there's several things I still can't remember. Why is that?" *Pawn to e5, I take his pawn.*

And for a second, I see a look of horror flash across my father's usually stoic face as he glances at the bloodied bandage on my left ear. *Knight to g4.* He must feel some remorse for what he's made me do to myself.

"Yeah, look what you made me do. Are you pleased with yourself?" I turn my head to give him a better look at Amy's surgical prowess and my self-stitching skills. *Knight to f3, I stay aggressive.*

"Benjamin. If you only knew . . . " *Knight to c6, he mirrors my move.*

"If I only knew what? That you wiped that poor girl's memory over and over again?" *Bishop to f4, I prepare for his offensive.*

"If only you knew the tru—" *Bishop to b4, he puts me in check, as expected.*

"The truth. Then tell me, Dad. Director Brew. I've got top-secret clearance, so I'm pretty sure there's nothing you can't tell me at this point. Or is this one of those need-to-know-basis type deals? Because that worked when I was a teenager, but in case you forgot, Dad, it's my fortieth birthday today. If you're not willing to tell me as an employee, at least look into your heart to tell me as a father to his son. Think about Amy. Your granddaughters. You put them all at risk when you wiped my memory." *Knight to d2, I cover up defensively, trying to bait him.*

"NO! YOU put them at risk when you came ranting in my office yesterday as the morality police," he says, stepping forward. *He takes the bait and exposes his queen, queen to e7.* "I wiped your memory because I thought it was the best way to protect Amy and the girls. To wipe out any memory you had of ever working for the agency. That's how bad you were raving yesterday, Benjamin. Saying stuff that could have gotten you . . . killed. Yes, your face tells me you're beginning to understand. I was protecting you."

The director has an excellent poker face, and I'm having trouble believing he has my best interests in mind. He played my dad for decades and I had no inkling he worked for the agency. It was nice that he sent me a text before my med school graduation letting me know he was appointed director before the press release came out the next day.

That was an interesting weekend. To realize that I had been surrounded by secrets my whole life. My dad was a professor of neuroscience. Dr. Brew got his PhD at Baylor and then taught at the University of Alabama in Birmingham until he joined the agency. So for most of my childhood, while I thought he was teaching, he was actually working in espionage. I realized that graduation weekend in 2005 that I had been under constant watch my whole life. That all my dad's talk of watching my behavior, of integrity, of doing the right thing when no one was looking was a little ridiculous, since someone was *always* looking. Even in college, when I didn't know my dad was in the agency, and I snuck off to do things without my parents' knowledge, Dad always seemed to know where I was. Come to think of it, I got away with nothing at Harvard. Dad would conveniently seem to call me right when I arrived at the loc—

Wait. It can't be. No, no, no.

"Dad . . . I bet you don't know what it's like to wake up feeling eighteen years old on your fortieth birthday. It's awful. I don't recommend it. But for that to happen, someone had to put that chip—yeah, the one in my earchunk on ice at home—someone had to put that chip into my ear on the night of my eighteenth birthday. Any ideas?" *I go back on the offensive, pawn to a3. I'll have him in check soon.*

His face answers the question. Wow. My own dad. It's all beginning to make sense, though. Dad was a neuroscience professor. He's the one that got me hooked up with Professor Chang at Harvard. He must have known about the chip. So he experimented on his own son. *Nice, Dad.*

"You know, Dad, the one problem with that first-gen chip? It's a little buggy. Buzzes when erasing memory and triggers a hell of a headache. But activated after dormant for twenty-two years? Pretty impressive. You must have been surprised it actually worked."

He can hardly look me in the eye at this point. "Benjamin, there's nothing I can say to make you forgive me for that act of selfishness. I . . . I wanted to protect you. Chips were limited at that point. I thought it would come in handy someday should the military ever deploy you. You were on the verge of signing your ROTC contract the next day. I did it myself, there's no one else to blame."

"Is that your way of saying 'I'm sorry'? Wow, you're out of practice, Dad. And are you going to apologize to all those soldiers who involuntarily have chips in their ears like me? Or Carrie?"

"It's not that simple, Benjamin. And you'd know that, but your memory still isn't completely back." My dad turns back to the mainframe. *Knight to ge5. He retreats, I've got him on defense.*

"Yeah, why is that? I removed the stupid chip." *Pawn to b4, I take his lonely bishop. My next move could cripple him.* "How could it possibly sti—"

Oh, crap. *Smothered mate, queen's pawn. Knight D3. Checkmate. I never saw it coming.*

I must have another chip.

Chapter 25

1430

When I was ten years old, we had a pet Maltese poodle named Princess. I remember begging my dad for a dog a million times. He didn't think my brother and I would ever be responsible enough to care for a pet. But we cared for that dog to the best of our ability. I was crushed when I found her dead in the middle of the road after owning her for only three months. I swore I had closed the gate after taking her for a walk before school. My older brother even vouched for me. Years later, when I was in medical school, my dad admitted that my mom might have forgotten to lock the gate after letting the dog out at lunch. We were never allowed to have a pet after that. Why withhold that information for fifteen years, leave me feeling bad for my dog's death for so long? Because that's the kind of person my dad is. He'd say he was protecting my mom, that those were the early stages of her Alzheimer's. That the dog meant as much to Mom as it did to me, but it was much better for the family if I took the blame. Ah, memory is a bitch. Pun intended.

"You son of a b@#%*! YOU PUT IN ANOTHER CHIP?" I point incredulously at my right ear. I can't believe it. Now I'm inches away from my father's face. He's still in pretty good shape for being sixty-seven. He doesn't budge even though I'm close enough to smell his aftershave.

"Benjamin. Look for yourself. I haven't been tampering with your memories."

He steps to the side of the console to allow me access. I use my thumbprint to log into my account. My father and I are the only two with accounts, but we each distrust the other. Once I'm in, I begin scanning my files.

Behind me he says, "The truth is in the memories, Benjamin," sounding confident, as if he already knows the truth I'm about to find.

My heart drops into my stomach as I find what I'm looking for. A file on myself. On activity concerning a second-gen chip. The entries go back a couple years.

I hear my dad sniggering behind me, clearly amused by my painful journey down memory lane.

"In case you don't remember how this works," he manages to say while chortling, "someone inputs the time frame they want deleted from the chip-bearer's memory."

I don't need him to finish the explanation but he continues to talk. *I designed the freaking chip, jerk.* I know that at night, around three A.M., the chip activates and targets the desired time frame. It's not always exact, sometimes removing too much or too little. It's also very dependent on the user. The chip works best during REM sleep, so if the user doesn't get adequate sleep, the memory wipe isn't as ... clean. The chip works best if the memories targeted happened within a day or two of erasure. The further away from the incident, the harder it is to wipe the memory. The newest chip was like taking a scalpel to the hippocampal memory bank. Chip 1.0? A sledgehammer.

As quickly as I tuned him out I hear his voice again. "The human brain is brilliant—days after an event, synapses continue to solidify the memories. Of course there's a critical point when the brain starts to prune away those old memories. But enough . . . do you have your answer yet?"

I've been looking while my dad's been talking to me, and I don't like what I see. Multiple entries. Over the past two years. As recently as yesterday. But the login signature is the same for every entry. Every freaking entry for the last three years. The same douchebag.

Me.

I'm feeling angrier than I've ever felt in my life. Anger quickly turns to embarrassment. I've been wiping my memory for years? Of what, though? And now I realize what those diary entries Amy showed me earlier were. They weren't serial numbers. I used the simplest code in the book. The numbers read backwards were just times I wanted deleted. I wrote them down in case I wanted to go back and bring those memories back, or if I didn't immediately have time to input them before leaving work.

Irony is that I don't remember the day I got chipped for apparently the second time. Which means either I had someone else do it for me so I wouldn't remember putting it in, or I've somehow suppressed the memory of the implantation. I'm hoping it's the former, but then that means there must even be some suppression of setting that up going on here. It would have to have been done by someone I trusted immensely at the agency, and that person doesn't exist. So I must have done it myself. And I suspect that because I had two active chips at once, one being deactivated has screwed up my brain in some way today. Because it seems like a pretty important freaking detail to remember, the day I put a chip in myself. I'm preparing to blame my dad when he attacks me with a flurry of questions.

"Do you want to know what you've been erasing all these years, Benjamin? Do you want to know the whole truth? Or is it best buried in that chip? I can't answer that question for you. But I'm pleading with you. I'm warning you. If you activate that chip and bring those memories back—and remember what we discussed in that meeting yesterday—I can't promise you how I'll respond.

"I'm so pleased you had the sense to delete our conversation yesterday. You have more sense than I give you credit for. After all, you are my son." He reaches out as if to put a comforting hand on my shoulder, but the fire in my eyes must give him second thoughts. "It's only a matter of minutes before the agents you disabled sound the alarm and find us here. I can protect you—or be forced to put you down. I have to protect our national interests. That's what's at stake here. Are you ready to fight this battle?"

But I've already made up my mind: now I have to know. My gut tells me that some wrongs need to be righted. And I'm the only one that can do it, so I need to know right now.

I scroll to the top of the page and hit Select All. I don't hesitate. I click the Undo button.

Nothing happens. The machine seems to pause for a split second before asking me if I'm sure. I know this has to be done. I click "OK."

Instantly, I feel the entire room spinning. I want to throw up. I do throw up. A lot. I'm on my hands and knees now. If my dad wanted me subdued, now would be the time. I feel completely defenseless. My breath is shallow and I'm beginning to panic. I'm trying to tell myself to breathe deeply, slowly, but the room has started to go black. And at the second I'm about to go, everything stops. The spinning. My breathing. A single tear forms in my eye and begins to make its way down my cheek.

But I'm not going to pass out.

I'm fine now.

And I remember everything. For a second time.

Chapter 26

1432

This must be what President Truman felt when he realized the devastation caused by the dropping of the atomic bombs. He couldn't have had any idea of the true destruction. He didn't watch the bombing live from the Oval Office. And even if he could have somehow, the extent of the destruction wouldn't be known for days, weeks . . . years. Truman simply weighed the pros and cons, made a phone call, and ordered the destruction of Hiroshima and Nagasaki. I can only imagine the number of times he thought back to that moment when he made the decision to go nuclear, and I wonder whether he regretted it, thought there might be another way, even though at the moment he believed his actions were for the greater good.

The greater good.

I am President Truman. I had this second-gen chip placed in my ear, and it was my idea to place it in the ears of soldiers without their knowledge or permission. For the good of the country. For the good of those soldiers. The greater good. Chang didn't want to, but we'd already put a chip in him, so we just made him forget some of those conversations. That was my idea, too. I had voluntarily erased my memory of doing these things. Because I knew they were wrong? Because I didn't want those decisions on my conscience—or in my conscious mind? Once we'd had a little success implanting the chip with people's consent, I was ok with the involuntary implantation because dumb soldiers would fear the chip for all the wrong reasons, not because it could protect their minds, their emotions.

Maybe they were right to be afraid.

When I began to see the destruction that this tiny chip was causing (and could cause?), I began to erase my own memory, the memories of my poor choices. Would President Truman have made a different decision if he'd known the extent of the damage that would be done not just to military targets, but to civilians as well?

I am not President Truman. I am not a man of integrity, and I certainly am not responsible for the day-to-day decisions that keep this nation safe. That's someone else's job—but even I question whether it's being done well.

Once I saw how eager the president was to use the chip in *his own daughter*, I became suspicious. I started to pry. Just how far would he go? It wasn't until I came to speak with the director yesterday that I knew. My father intimated that he and the president had discussed placing chips into people other than soldiers. Foreign dignitaries staying at our embassy. Other unsuspecting world leaders who had stayed in the White House or on US soil. If this information ever got out, that they had followed through with this dangerous idea, it would be World War III. This would make WikiLeaks look like a local gossip column.

This is what I confronted the director, my dad, over. This is what I was raving mad about. It's not what I designed the chip for. This could bring down the whole agency, our diplomatic relations with other countries, world peace. No joke. World peace was at stake. We're at the brink of war with the Chinese, and this would be "the chip that broke the camel's tooth."No, I didn't actually say that when talking with my dad, but that morsel of eloquent prose would have really diffused the tension. I thought if I was dramatic enough, my dad and the president would realize their folly and back down. I think that's why I erased the memory of our conversation—because I believed I had gotten through to them, and the thought that my chip would be misused in this way gave me an ulcer. Clearly, I wasn't convincing—otherwise my dad wouldn't have erased twenty-two years of memories to be safe. Or . . . they really were going to implant the chip in these foreign diplomats whether I liked the idea or not.

But then I'd had my big Truman moment. I'd clearly had several small Truman moments, given the number of times I'd wiped my own memory. Yesterday, I'd come to fully realize the pain my chip had caused—could cause—in the wrong hands. Exhibit A? Carrie. Missing so many doses of her medication that she could die. Exhibit B? The director and the president scheming to implant the chip in our friends and enemies. And yesterday, I wished I had never created the chip, never let it fall into government hands.

The problem with what my dad did to me is that he took away my choice. My choice to convince him or anyone else who'd listen that a plan to implant memory-wiping chips in our allies and adversaries was utterly dangerous. And illegal. And war-provoking. This wouldn't be a scandal that anyone could claim was the work of a few lower-level employees. The president of the United States was directly involved. And knowing what my dad did to me twenty-two years ago, implanting a chip without my consent? The Carrie issue is now even more personal.

So what choice do I really have? Keep my mouth shut and protect my family? Or protect the criminal behavior of the country I swore to defend against enemies foreign and domestic? I could swear allegiance to my father and make all this go away. But how could I live with myself, look the First Daughter—hell, my own daughters—in the eye? Carrie is just a pawn in this dangerous game of chess, but she's the pawn that made me realize the entire game board is at stake.

I'm still on my hands and knees over a pool of vomit. *Watch the French cuffs, Brew.* My father is beside me, shuffling his feet nervously. I think he's not sure if I'm breathing. I'm not, but he should know I can hold my breath for over three minutes, a skill I honed in our backyard pool over many summers. He leans over me. He's not going to like what happens next.

Like a seasoned wrestler, I reach up with my right hand and grab him around the neck. I leverage his weight easily, flipping him over my back and dropping his body with a dramatic thud on the floor, barely missing the vomit. With the breath knocked out of him, I place him in a sleeper hold, his legs wriggling like a pair of agitated king cobras.

I whisper "Trust me" into his ear as his eyes blink shut and his body goes limp. Like a good doctor, I dutifully check his carotid pulse before laying him flat on his back. I jump back to the mainframe and begin furiously clicking. Within a minute, I'm done.

I feel relieved, but there's no time to dwell on what I've done. I need to move.

I know my dad's agents will be on me any minute, which is why I ripped the gas mask off the agent I knocked out earlier. I put it on and begin yelling for help. I'm leaning over my dad as the first agents run in. They always come in threes, a result of my dad's policy directive based on the Biblical proverb that a triple-braided cord is more difficult to break. My first move is always to thin out that cord.

"Help me, he's been knocked out. I can't find a pulse," I say anxiously with a hand on my dad's neck. "You," I bark at the one on the far left, "get an AED just to be safe." The two other agents are quickly at my side, one checking Dad's radial pulse, the other making sure he's breathing. I feel bad taking advantage of people who are trying to help him, but I know he's going to be fine.

They might not be.

I believe in swift, nonlethal force. I don't want a long, drawn-out exchange; broken bones are acceptable.

It's easy enough to slam the head of the guard checking my father's breathing into the linoleum. If he's not out, he's deeply concussed. The one checking his pulse is completely caught off guard. The base of my open palm crushes the cartilage of his nose easily. He yelps and falls backwards, clutching at the blood pouring from his face. I'm on him in a flash, my arm around his neck quickly putting him down. *Sigh. There goes the shirt.*

Seconds later, I'm back in the hallway, heading towards the elevators. I discard the gas mask in a trash bin as I near the elevators. I'm in luck; someone is walking into the middle one as I arrive. I slip in quietly, using the ride up to center myself, straightening my collar and adjusting the ID badge that does not belong to me.

When the doors open, I quickly make my way to the lobby. Angela is just coming through the doors. I point towards the exit and she throws up her hands, exasperated.

"Do you know how hard it was to find parking on the first floor?" she asks angrily. "Something tells me you knew it would take me a while to find a space."

I shrug, which just seems to make her more upset. Once we are finally out of the building, I make brief eye contact with her and grin, as if to answer her question. She doesn't say a word as we get into the car and drive off site. With HQ in the rearview mirror, I finally allow my body to relax and look at my watch. Eight minutes and forty-five seconds. With time to spare . . .

Chapter 27

1446

Angela drives. We ride in silence. Two minutes, to be exact. I think she's waiting for me to tell her what happened, but I'm not ready to tell her I assaulted my dad after finding out he placed the first-generation chip in my ear and that I have another one inside me. And that the director has obviously been able to trace me since the beginning of this whole charade—though I may have fixed that problem at the mainframe for both me and Angela. I'm not really ready to tell her that she does have a chip, but I know the question is burning a hole in her . . . ear.

"Yes."

I know that one word is enough. There's a part of me that hopes she doesn't know what question I'm answering, but how could she not? With my memories back, all of them, I remember how Angela feels about me. I remember our conversation nine months ago about her father dying in a car accident when she was ten. I remember the way she looked at me when she told the story, the way I gave her space to mourn her father's death, even though it happened almost a decade ago. I remember her seemingly offhand comment a week later that I reminded her of him in some ways. Would my betrayal, chipping her involuntarily, be too much for her? I wonder if she'd wish I could remove her memory of the day her father died. No—she'd want to remember that day, because she told me that even though he was a serious man who couldn't even laugh at his own jokes, that day was one of his happiest. It was the day her mom told him the ultrasound showed that the baby in her belly was a boy. Angela's dad jumped for joy, then into his car to pick up a bottle of champagne from the liquor store three blocks away. He never made it. Angela probably hangs onto that precious memory, even though it skirts the edges of pain and misery. *What a dangerous, foolish game I've been playing with people's minds.*

I keep my eyes glued to the road while lost in my thoughts about Angela, but then I feel her eyes burning a hole in my cheek. She's driving, so her eyes *should* be burning a hole in the road we're on, so I'm a little worried. In my periphery, I see her lips moving . . . but I don't hear a sound. Is she mouthing words to me, or singing along to a song in her head? Or have I . . . have I lost my hearing?

And now I'm fully aware we're driving in complete silence. I shake my head vigorously, trying to reset my hearing.

Another five long seconds. Angela is punching me in the left arm now, her left hand still on the wheel, thankfully. She's probably wondering why I'm not responding to her. I turn to speak to her, but it's that feeling of being at a loud bar or concert and trying to talk to the person beside you when you can't hear your own voice. My voice is probably way too loud as I say, "I CAN'T HEAR YOU." As soon as I utter those words, I know I must sound like a pretty big jackass, because how could I NOT hear her? And then all of a sudden, my hearing is back. My ears hurt. Stone Temple Pilots' *Interstate Love Song* blares on the radio.

—r what I read between the lines
Your lies

Angela whips the wheel sharply to the right and we stop abruptly on the shoulder of I-64.

"What the hell was that?" Angela's yelling burns my sensitive ears. *What's the deal with ears today?*

I cover them with my hands and yell back, "Shut up for five seconds." I'm taking deep breaths and telling my brain to calm down.

Breathing is the hardest thing to do
With all I've said and all that's dead for you
You lied
Goodbye

My ears are hurting less. I uncover them and look Angela in the eye. "You're not going to believe me, but I haven't been able to hear anything you said for the last five minutes."

"You're right, Brew." She pauses. " I don't believe you."

It's the chip. I'm sure it's the chip. "I don't have time to explain, Angela. We've got to get to Carrie as soon as possible. But . . . but why are we headed back towards the hospital?" I point at the green interstate sign up ahead. I'd asked Angela to track down Carrie when she went to park the car, so I assumed we were heading to the ODU campus. "Are you ill?"

"That's funny. I was going to ask you the same thing," she responds with a nervous laugh. "Does that move work on your wife? The whole, 'I've lost my hearing, were you saying something important' act? She looks way too smart to fall for that. But I'm just a dumb college kid."

Promises of what I seemed to be
Only watched the time go by
All of these things I said to you

"Angela, FOR THE LOVE OF GOD, this is not the time to get your feelings hurt. Why are we headed back to Portsmouth Naval? ODU is in the other direction!"

She glances to her left as the Prius slowly gathers speed to re-enter traffic. "Because that's where Carrie is. I just pinged her locator and she's not in class like she's supposed to be. It's part of what I've been trying to tell you for the last five minutes. I think something bad happened."

Chapter 28

1515

Angela flashes her badge at the gate and we luck our way into a second-floor parking spot. As we take the walking bridge into the main hospital, I attempt to smooth things over.

"What happened in the car back there . . . have I ever done that to you before?"

We walk by the coffee shop and Angela makes a stutter step, as if she's going to stop for a beverage, then changes her mind; maybe because we have urgent business, maybe because she's caught off guard by my question.

"Actually, yeah. But not for five full minutes. There have been a few times, especially over the last six months, when I'm talking to you but you seem to not be listening." She nods at the guard at the quarterdeck as we walk briskly through the sliding doors. "I assumed you were just growing tired of me."

Amy has gotten on me for the same thing. I thought I was developing a touch of adult ADHD. But then I started having issues with my vision. The ophthalmologist found nothing on dilated exam, but he suggested if my complaints of complete blindness for several seconds increased, a brain scan might be warranted. I was afraid of what he might find on that scan, but now I'm pretty sure I'm putting it all together.

I absentmindedly summon the elevator while I explain my theory. "It's the chip. You have to understand, Angela. This second-generation chip—even though I did the vast majority of work on it during college and med school—wasn't officially ready for human deployment. We continued testing our mouse models for years. And like any medical device, once we proved it was safe, we'd be approved to move to human testing.

"But we never got that far becau— I started noticing irregularities in the mice's behavior. Running into walls during maze runs they had done dozens of times. Not responding to audio stimuli as they had previously. And while I wasn't able to prove it, I suspected the chip had something to with this. That the chip was somehow affecting the mice on a sensory level."

I fail to tell Angela my role in the chip program. In my head, I finish the sentence: *We never got that far because we skipped right to human testing, soldier testing.* I leave out the fact that even though I had the chip program shut down once I was concerned about the ethical implications of erasing memories, I was the one, with the director's urging, who revived the program a few years ago to begin covert human testing among soldiers—no doubt after testing it on myself and being pleased with the results. This would become part of my Nobel memoir. Hubris convinced me that many great scientists had tested their hypotheses on themselves. Why should I be any different? Soldiers are the perfect guinea pigs, I reasoned. They're government property. How many times during my field training did someone remind me of that? When you own something, you have the ability to know almost everything about it. We had almost every measurable we needed: height, weight, blood type, complete metabolic panel including liver function tests, complete blood count, lipid panel; heck, we even knew HIV status and whether or not a soldier had been treated for an STD. We had access to every prescription a soldier had ever received, plus the results of all random drug testing. Our database allowed us to access every medical visit, lab, x-ray, and test a soldier had had since 2005. Medically, Uncle Sam knows everything you've done, where you did it, and who you did it with.

This was better than breeding transgenic mice. We simply handpicked soldiers who fit the profile we wanted to test. We weren't looking to cure disease, as Chang had set out to do from the onset. No, the government was looking to protect its assets. Protecting soldiers from PTSD meant you could deploy them multiple times without fear of burnout, psychiatric scars. If you wiped out the memory of a short deployment, would soldiers really miss their families? If you wiped out the memory of a traumatic gun battle, would soldiers fear returning to combat? We had so many questions, and the only way to answer them was to implant the chip and observe.

So we created our first team of super-soldiers, ten healthy men and women recruited for an elite special-operations team. We followed them for about a year.

After year one, the director had seen enough. Seven successful missions, no PTSD, no reported side effects. The soldiers were happy, reported feeling fresh, and were eager to return to the field. The director authorized the immediate production of a hundred more microchips. (The chips are incredibly expensive. For every five created, the Pentagon had to remove one stealth bomber from the budget.) Of course, the director didn't tell the Ways and Means Committee the true nature of the chip and how we got our results. We deflected the ethical questions that were sure to arise by overwhelming them with charts and graphs that highlighted our successes. The committee showed restraint and wisely only approved thirty chips.

I didn't know the extent of the director's use of the first-gen chip. Now I know he was using them as early as 1998. If he'd implanted them into soldiers back then, I didn't know anything about it.

When the elevator doors open on the fifth floor, Angela steps out before me. I'm staring at the back of her head hoping my hearing is back to normal when I hear her ask, "How do you even know she's on this floor, Brew? She could be anywhere in the hospital."

I point to the sign in front of us. "Because if the director had his way today, this is where he'd have stashed me."

And with that, we enter the psych ward.

Chapter 29

1520

I don't consider myself a liar; I'm simply very good at withholding information. But eventually this will catch up with me. Like in a couple of minutes.

Carrie is in the psych ward because of what I did back at HQ, when I was fiddling with the mainframe after disabling my father. Not only was I deactivating my own microchip, but I was also deactivating the First Daughter's.

I probably didn't think that through very well. What if Carrie had been driving, swimming, operating heavy machinery? Having those memories flood in could have been fatal. On second thought, maybe I did think things through. Given that I deactivated her chip midday, she was probably in class. She never drove herself anywhere (Secret Service did that for her), and under their watchful eye, it was fairly difficult for her to get hurt.

Carrie undoubtedly experienced the same side effects I did (disorientation, vomiting), but probably fared considerably worse. She isn't in the great physical shape I am in, and just peeing in a cup makes her squeamish. Since I'm her doctor, I'm well aware of her health issues, and she has some notable ones.

Let's start with her juvenile myoclonic epilepsy. She's been on antiepileptic medicine since age nine. The First Daughter, like many young adults, has trouble remembering to take her medication consistently and doesn't want to be treated like a child; but noncompliance in her case means seizures, so per her father's orders, her Secret Service unit reminds her often. She hates being reminded to take her meds, but she hates even more how they make her feel. She's tried several medications and settled on Topamax a few years ago, but the effects on her memory and cognition have increased with her dosage. "Dopamax" is no joke. At our last visit, Carrie begged me to talk to her neurologist about changing medications or eliminating Topamax altogether. "I feel fine," she told me. "Why do I take a medication that makes me feel dopey? I'd rather just have a seizure . . . they last less than forty-five seconds and I'm usually fine within five minutes."

But in my mind, and in her dad's mind, epilepsy is the least of Carrie's problems. Synthetic marijuana is a far more dangerous demon to slay, and in some ways, that one is Angela's fault.

Chapter 30

1522

It's been said that kids don't have drug problems; they have drug solutions. "Spice" was Carrie's solution to her anxiety, a problem that likely predated her epilepsy. She was introduced to synthetic marijuana at a party during her freshman year. Angela told me it was an accident—some kids were passing around a blunt, Carrie wanted to try something she'd never tried before, and Angela couldn't stop her (and has felt guilty about it ever since).

Can you imagine being eighteen and employed by the leader of the free world? And he forbids you to allow his daughter to get high, to get pregnant, or end up dead? And two weeks into college she's accomplished one of the three? But like everything today, it comes back to the issue of control: the president trying to control his daughter. The director (and me) trying to control memory.

And now we see the fruits of our labor. Chaos nips at the fingertips of control. Try to gain a tighter grasp? Chaos shatters the object into a million pieces, like a glass ornament in the hands of a toddler. Loosen your grip? Chaos, like a wet soap bar, makes your fingers slippery, and you never regain control.

We tried both with Carrie. More security, then less-direct observation. And then the president put the pressure on. Carrie was elusive even with Angela, finding opportunities to buy and smoke spice under the many watchful eyes assigned to her. If the most powerful teenager in the world could pull this off, what chance do parents of regular teenagers have?

That was not a pleasant day at the office six months ago, standing around my father's desk with the president on speakerphone:

"What the hell? How hard is it to protect my daughter from that poison? Does she need a new doctor? A new Secret Service detail? A new teenage friend on my payroll who can do a better job of helping her say 'no' to drugs?"

The anger in his voice sent chills down my spine. With the push of a few buttons, the man on the other end of the line could order tactical strikes to control an Iraqi insurgent uprising on the other side of the globe, but he couldn't control his own upstart eighteen-year-old daughter.

"Mr. President," I'd said, "this is very challenging. Carrie has proven to be very resourceful and may have been using this stuff prior to your presidency. I think her connections to spice run deeper than we even imagined." I realized this information was probably not going to be comforting.

"Oh, so you're saying this could blow up in our faces in the press? 'President's junkie daughter likely high during presidential campaign.' I need you to fix this, Benjamin. It's why I hired you. You're supposed to be good with teenagers. The best. This is your best?"

He certainly knew all the buttons to push. My father looked away from me, shaking his head. *You too, Dad?* And then I said the words that now threaten the very integrity and security of our great republic:

"Why not implant a chip and teach her to forget her drug habit?"

Silence. The director's head swiveled back to me, his eyes wide with intrigue, the corners of his lips eagerly twitching upwards. I continued.

"The chip we use in our highly successful spec-ops team. What if we placed a chip in Carrie's ear? Every time she uses the drug—and I think we have a good idea of when she might be using; we certainly know right *after* she has used—every time she uses, we erase that portion of her memory. Eventually, she'll forget the highs. She'll still have cravings, yes, but they should decrease as she has no recollection of getting high."

More silence. I feared I'd overstepped my boundary. I'd just suggested that we weaponize the president's daughter. Because that's what the chip really is: a weapon. It's a tiny implantable stealth bomber that can make an average soldier more dangerous, more durable. And now I was suggesting we place it in a young woman who's lost her way, lost control. I was suggesting we harness the control she's lost by manipulating her memory.

Looking the part of a king in his swivel chair, my dad folded his hands in his lap. And smiled.

We awaited the president's response. The speakerphone buzzed softly.

"Do it."

Then the line went dead.

Chapter 31

1523

Angela grabs my right arm before I walk through the double doors of 5B. "So you're saying Carrie went crazy today and you knew this would happen? Because this is where the director would have placed you? Because . . . "

And then her face goes blank as she cradles her forehead in her hands. She gets it.

"Because Carrie has a microchip as well," she states, "and it's effed up her head like yours today. Her handlers see her freaking out, so they bring her to the most secure ward in the hospital. So does Carrie think she's twelve years old or something? This should be hilarious."

I push the button that connects us to the intercom at the nurses' station. This is a locked ward. "Let me come clean," I say while pinching the bridge of my nose to hide my eyes and what little pride I have left. "I'm the reason Carrie has a chip. It was my idea. And without going into details—yes, we are talking about something way outside of your security clearance—the chip was supposed to save Carrie's li—"

"5B nurses' desk. How may I assist you?"

I clear my throat. "Um, yes, this is Dr. Brew, I'm here to see one of my patients." The inflection in my voice at the end of that statement makes me sound like I'm asking for permission.

"Last name, please."

"Banning." It's just a name, but it's not. Under the current circumstances, uttering "Banning" on a psych ward is like yelling "fire" in a movie theater. It's dangerous ... and I know what will follow is enhanced security protocol—Carrie's agents are sure to be on high alert. They aren't expecting visitors.

"Are we just going to walk in?" Angela reaches into her jacket to secure her weapon. "You haven't exactly told me the plan, and I don't think Jim and Terry are just going to let us walk out of here with Carrie in tow."

Angela's right. There's little chance that Carrie's handlers will let her out of their sight. But I have one huge advantage today: the letters after my name. MD. These agents are on my turf.

There's a click at the door. I reach for the handle but a voice behind us stops me dead in my tracks.

"Whoa there, cowboy. Place your hands on your head and turn around slowly."

Chapter 32

1522

Ah, the best-laid plans. Perhaps the dose of sodium thiopental I slipped my dad while he lay on the floor of Level -1 was too low. He's woken up and called the cavalry. We're done. Carrie was the key to fixing a great deal of today's mess. I felt if I could just talk to her about the chip, about the mistakes we made, then she could appeal to her dad, and he would shut the program down once and for all. We could give the soldiers back their memories. All would be right in the world.

But now I'm not going to get the chance. By the end of the day, I could be in Leavenworth or Guantanamo. What did I miss? I thought I planned this well. Well *enough.* Hearing Terry's southern drawl behind me was the last thing I expected. I turn around slowly, hands on my head, shoulders slumped in defeat. Angela does the same.

And then I see the look on Terry's face.

"Gotcha, Doc!" His right index finger points at my midsection, his left index finger doing the same to Angela. "Just messin' with you. I hope you brought something special for Carrie because that girl is all kind of crazy today."

Nothing like a Secret Service agent with a sense of humor. I'm not amused, but I feel a lot better than I did ten seconds ago. Terry Cummings is wearing black denim jeans, a black turtleneck, and a thin black jacket that bulges prominently where his weapon is holstered. I flip him the bird and turn back to the ward door purposefully before it locks. "Is she that bad?" I say, following Terry and Angela through the open door.

"She's an eight on the crazy meter. My meter only goes to eight, so that's pretty high." Terry walks in front of me shaking his head. We head towards the private rooms at the end of the hall, to the right. The psych ward is divided into two sections: one for civilian dependents of military members and one for active-duty military. The active-duty military section is frequently full. It's not easy being in the military. It will mess with your head. Most of the patients are trainees: young adults, many fresh out of high school. Their buffer for coping with stress is very thin. When your resilience is low, nothing gets you a ticket home faster than saying you want to hurt yourself. So while there are some on the psych ward attempting to manipulate the system, the vast majority need real help.

As we walk down the hall, I see Jim Lannigan, Terry's partner, outside the last room on the left. I read the names on the doors as I walk by—and stop abruptly. Angela narrowly avoids bumping into me.

"Siaw-Lattey . . . I know that name," I whisper.

It would be hard to forget. It's a Ghanaian name. Ghana—my grandparents' country of origin before they emigrated here in the sixties. I have a lot of family still in Ghana, so when I recruited Kwasi Siaw-Lattey two years ago, he was memorable to me for many reasons.

"This is one of my guys," I say. "Can I stop in here for a minute? I'll catch up to you." Terry nods and beckons Angela to continue following him. She makes no effort to move, and worry drapes her face. I step closer and whisper in her ear.

"Just make small talk and keep her calm. She'll be happy to see you. I'll be right in." She smiles weakly and turns to follow Terry.

I turn back to Siaw-Lattey's hospital room, ready to face my fear. Why is one of the most elite soldiers from our special-ops, chip-implanted test group on the psychiatry ward? I'm not sure I really want to know.

Chapter 33

1525

Kwasi lies motionless on his hospital bed. His eyes are open, staring into space. His skin looks ashen, his face gaunt. He looks like he weighs no more than 120 pounds, his green gown draped lifelessly over his body like oversized doll clothing. This is not the super-soldier I trained two years ago. I take two cautious steps towards my soldier's bed.

"Kwasi, it's Brew. How are you?"

No response. I step closer, trying to get into his line of sight. His eyes don't move, his normally white sclera slightly yellow, perhaps a sign of early liver failure. I wave a hand over his face. Again, nothing. His facial hair grows in indiscriminate patches and I take note of the crumbs in his beard, glancing at his largely untouched lunch tray. I take small steps backwards, making an about-face to place myself squarely in front of the computer. I wave my hospital badge over the terminal and it hums to life. Within seconds, I'm accessing Kwasi's medical record.

He's been an inpatient for the last six months, during which his body has been slowly shutting down. He's blind, but his eyes seem to work fine when tested by ophthalmology. He has lost 80% of his hearing—though his ear bones tested normal in last week's audiology report. In medicine, we talk about central versus peripheral deficits often. Some babies have trouble breathing when they contract respiratory syncytial virus, or RSV. They can become so sick they stop breathing, but RSV's impact is peripheral: it affects the lungs and airways, not the brain. Other babies, usually premature ones, can stop breathing for central reasons: their brain, which is central to their breathing, doesn't tell them to take a breath. Their lungs work just fine, but their brains sometimes need prescription caffeine or breathing devices that remind them to breathe.

Kwasi is like the latter. His brain is the problem, not his peripheral organs. His eyes and ears would function normally on anyone else's body, but his brain is shutting down, and there's no doubt in my mind our microchip is the culprit. All those senses integral to creating and consolidating memories? Severely compromised because of our chip.

So these are the long-term effects I never got to see. This is what my father was willing to hide from me, or wasn't willing to wait to see. While I was visiting wounded warriors who were making successful transitions because of the chip, my father was hiding the test cases from me. I just assumed those troops were still in deep cover, doing missions, or getting a much-deserved break. But now I'm convinced my father knows that Kwasi is here and very sick. And if Kwasi is here, then there are others.

"Brew, is that you? I'd recognize that smell of Old Spice and overconfidence anywhere."

"I think you mean 'Old Spice and overconfidence anywhere, *sir.*' I still outrank you, soldier."

"Ha! 'Outrank,' my butt. I'm going to pretend I didn't hear you say that—though it's not that hard to pretend. Speak a little louder." Kwasi struggles to sit up on his elbows and I lend him a hand. He jumps when I touch him, as if my fingers are covered in acid. I recoil as he gingerly rubs his skin. He seems to be looking in my general direction but I can tell he's just trying to locate me based on sound (and smell, apparently).

I don't have much time to talk. "Kwasi, I'm so sorry," I begin. "And I know that doesn't mean much right now, but I feel responsible for the state you're in. I will do everything in my power to make this right."

He shrugs. "Can you fix Alexander, too? And Fitch? Coffner isn't blind yet, but she's lost more hearing than the rest of us. At least our families are taken care of. Oh wait, I don't really have one so you don't have to worry about that. I don't know what the hell you did to us, but I'm kind of wishing I had never answered my phone when you called that day a few years ago." This knifes through me like a blade through soft butter. I am melting on the inside, and I fear it's the special hell I've created for myself by the lives I've destroyed. CS Lewis convinced me in *The Great Divorce* that hell is the absence of God. I feel empty right now, and I'm not even sure Kwasi's forgiveness can fill the chasm I created.

"I will make this right. Believe me." My voice lacks conviction as I feel a chill run down my spine. "I . . . will . . . make . . . this . . . right."

With that, I turn and walk out of his room. There is nothing more to say.

Now comes the doing.

Chapter 34

1529

Angela is sitting on the end of Carrie's bed when I walk in. Jim and Terry share a laugh just outside of the room, finding humor in something on Jim's cell phone. I close the door behind me, though I'm aware the agents can still see us through the large window in the door. When Carrie's eyes finally meet mine, all I see is her anger.

"What have you done to me?" she seethes through gritted teeth.

I don't know what to say because I don't know how much Angela has told her in the short time they've been together. No surprise. I sometimes forget Angela is an adolescent, a young adult. Developmentally, the relationships she forms at this stage in her life are deep and meaningful. There is a fierce loyalty—and even though it's her job, Angela, like any other young adult, can't separate duty from emotion. It's probably why she felt bad trying to drug me.

It's probably why I didn't feel so bad doing the things I've done over the past several years. Like putting a chip in her best friend. Like putting a chip in Angela. And I can rationalize that I've done it all to protect them, but at some point, I have to face the truth: I am selfish and wrong to have done these things without their consent.

"Carrie," I begin, "I feel terrible for what you've experienced today." I've been saying sorry quite a bit today. This probably won't be the last time. "Angela's told you about the chip, I'm sure." She nods slowly. "I don't know how much she told you, but we thought—I thought—that we could use the chip to . . . to help you stop smoking spice."

Carrie slams her fist on the bed and Angela and I recoil. "That's BS! I haven't smoked spice for over five months! Yeah, I've had some weed from time to time, and Doc, I know the difference. The highs are way different. And I'm really trying to smoke less weed, for a lot of reasons. So I have no idea where you're getting your information from. You're supposed to be my doctor. I tell you everything. How can you of all people not believe me?"

I don't want to make her feel any worse than she already does, but I have science on my side, and this is an argument she's not going to win. But it should keep the argument brief so I can get to the point—that I need her to talk to her dad about shutting down the chip program. I point out the multiple positive drug screens I've received over the past several months, and as recently as last week. I point out the behavior reports filed by Jim and Terry, the people around her the most. Their detailed descriptions of her use, and the great lengths Carrie has gone to to hide it. She looks more confused the more I talk. I begin to describe one of their most recent reports when Angela interrupts me.

"Brew, I was with Carrie all day that day. The time you allege she used? We were at the White House. With her dad. It's just not possible."

"Maybe I have the days wrong. How did you explain th—"

"The positive tests? Doctor Brew, I have no idea. I have no recollection of submitting that many urine samples. But you have to believe me. I think . . . I think I'm being set up."

I deal with substance abuse in adolescents on a regular basis. I would like to believe I've seen everything at this point. Every ruse used to convince me—the medical professional—that the patient does not have a problem with drugs. *I'm being set up by the Secret Service* is a new one, though. I shake my head in disbelief. "Carrie, you know I'm your biggest fan. I just find it hard to bel—"

"That someone would erase my memories without my permission?"

Touché.

One of the things I'm trained to do as a doctor is develop a differential diagnosis: a list of all the conditions that a particular set of symptoms could point to. I have to consider all options in this situation. I do trust Carrie, and even when she was using spice, she always told me when she did it. So why would she be lying now, in this specific circumstance? This is why relationship with a patient is so vital. Carrie isn't a number to me. She's like one of my children. I treat her medically as a patient, but emotionally, she's like one of my daughters. So when she tells me to trust her, I need to listen. And to broaden my differential.

"Carrie, the worst part of all this is that I feel like I've put your life in danger. I fear some of the memories we erased caused you to miss doses of your Topamax. Sometimes you probably even took extra doses. I wouldn't be able to live with myself if you seized because we were tampering with your memory. The right thing to do would have been to confront the issue head on. To talk to you about drug use. I'm sure your dad tried to. He's always passionate when he brings it up."

Carrie laughs out loud for a full ten seconds. Angela and I stare at her, not sure how to react. "That's the funniest thing I've ever heard. The last time Dad and I talked about drugs was about five months ago, when I'd actually completely stopped using! About the only thing he and I have been talking about consistently over the last few months is . . . OMG."

The dramatic pause has Angela and me on our heels, and I realize I'm holding my breath. Carrie's memories are back. If there's something else going on, she'll remember it now.

"I know exactly why Dad's been erasing my memories," she whispers, tears welling up in her eyes, unable to hide her disappointment . . . and fear. "We've got to get out of here. Now."

Chapter 35

1532

What Carrie tells us turns everything on its head. If she's telling the truth—and I can't see how she'd make this up to cover up her drug abuse—then we have a huge problem on our hands.

And by we, I mean our country. Our global community. My worst fears have been realized. The conversation with my dad yesterday? A sham. Our hypothetical talk about what would happen if chips were implanted in our allies or enemies? Not so hypothetical.

So the drug tests . . . fake? The detailed reports . . . fabricated? Those erased memories . . . those times I thought we were erasing drug-fueled highs . . . were actually conversations with her dad. And if what Carrie alleges is true, it's even more than that. Maybe we erased moments when agents were listening in as she spoke with friends or even to herself. Carrie says she rehearsed the conversation she would have with her dad a million times in her bathroom mirror. A room that is likely miked up. All the agents would have to do is review the footage, then erase anything that concerned them.

But there's no time to sit here and ponder the deception. I know I've been deceived, but I'm one to talk. Carrie's right. We need to get out right now while there's time. Once my dad knows that Carrie is fully operational, the full force of the agency will descend upon us. And it's at that moment that I realize my current plan, the plan to go to President Daddy Dearest and appeal to his human side, would fail. Miserably.

The new plan is much simpler: Run.

My eyes meet Angela's. She nods at me and springs into action. Before I know it, she's at the door, beckoning the agents into the room. I grab Terry before he enters and pull him aside. "Kid's had a rough day. She's finally calming down."

The door is still open, and out of the corner of my eye I see Angela engaging Jim. She's giggling and playing cute. Jim has a weakness for attractive women, especially ones half his age. Terry's facing me so his back is to the open door. It's only been about thirty seconds, but that's all we need. I see Angela motioning for Jim to follow her to the bathroom, looking concerned. A loud click grabs Terry's attention and he swivels around. "Where's Carrie?" he asks, peering into the room.

"Oh, she's in the bathroom with Angela and Jim. The toilet wouldn't stop making this gurgling noise—Jim can't resist a home improvement project, even if it's not his own home."

"Tell me about it," Terry says, rolling his eyes. "He'd only been at our house for about five minutes last week when I found him caulking my bathtub. Scary part is, I don't even have caulk in my house!"

We share a deep belly laugh and I excuse myself, telling Terry I need to run to the nurses' station to make sure all the orders are properly written for Carrie's admission. I have no idea how long our ruse will last. My guess is Terry will maintain his position outside of the room per protocol. Jim will eventually realize that the toilets here are just loud and gurgly, and have been for the last ten years. Angela will stall as long as she can and then the two of them will emerge from the bathroom. I turned off Carrie's monitor before I left her room, so as I walk by the nurses' station, I tell her nurse she's fine and just using the bathroom. She buzzes me out of the ward and I sprint to the staircase.

Carrie almost blew it. As she snuck out of her room and through the badge-activated back door ten feet away, she let the heavy door close louder than I would have liked. But even if Terry thinks someone went out that door, how could it be Carrie? She doesn't have a badge. Or does she?

Luckily, I don't need my badge between the psych ward and my office, where I told Carrie to meet me. Angela will feign ignorance, tell the agents not to freak out, suggest that she might be with her nurse in the treatment room getting blood drawn. This will take no more than ninety seconds. Agents are efficient and they know the critical window of time it takes for a target to escape. Every second is precious. All I know is that we probably have four minutes to get off the hospital base before the Secret Service orders a lockdown, and I honestly don't think we can make it out that quickly. It would take us that long to get to the car, and when the hospital is locked down, everything closes—the parking garage, the gate, everything except the emergency room.

So for the second time today, it's an emergency to get out of the hospital. Oh, the irony.

I'm sprinting down the hall of the pediatric clinic and nearly run over Carrie. "I got a little lost, sorry."

"You did well, Carrie," I say, "but we need to keep moving." During my run down the stairs two or three steps at a time, I had plotted out our next move. Only two locations make sense: *The Virginian Pilot*'s editorial office and the Chinese consulate.

So as I pull Carrie down the hall towards the emergency exit I escaped by earlier, I do something I know is wrong, something worse than yelling "fire" in a crowded movie theater.

I pull the fire alarm.

Chapter 36

1544

You know what you can't do in the middle of a fire drill? Call a Code Green. At Portsmouth Naval Hospital, a Code Green means a patient is missing, because patients wear hospital-issued green gowns. It triggers a lockdown and a description of the patient blares overhead. If Secret Service calls a Code Green—and is desperate enough to not only describe Carrie Banning in detail but say her name—she'll be recognizable by 75% of the people in the hospital.

But a fire has the opposite effect. It means everybody needs to get out of the hospital. Well, mostly everyone. Critically ill patients and infants generally shelter in place until the risk is properly assessed. So I feel terrible, but this is the only way I can be sure we'll be able to get out. It will create a great deal of confusion, which will buy us even more time.

Carrie and I are at the Prius in three and a half minutes. As we exit the garage, I see security guards and uniformed seamen ushering men, women, and children out of the hospital into the cold. I feel awful; I want to cry. Doctors don't do crap like this. Jackass teenagers and angry, immature—and sometimes mentally unstable—navy corpsmen who don't feel like working for a few hours do this. But we're almost to the

145

gate, which means in a few seconds I won't have to worry about what I've done.

Except that I see military police running out of the gate security stand to seal off the exit. *No!* Jim and Terry must be on to me. I swerve away from the gate and head for the east side of the hospital, towards the emergency room. There is one trick left up my sleeve.

I pull into the first parking space I see and tell Carrie to get out. I look across the bay at downtown Norfolk. A ferry across the water would be nice, but the ferry leaves from somewhere else. One of the most intriguing features of Portsmouth Naval is that the admiral of the hospital actually lives in a house on the hospital campus. It's a beautiful old two-story Colonial Revival, built in the fifties.

I'm standing in the ER parking lot surveying the scene, trying to make my decision. I've broken a crapload of rules today and I need to break one more, but I'm weighing the cost. There's an ambulance humming to my left, keys still in the ignition, the driver and his EMT partner loading their elderly patient onto a gurney and about to wheel him into the hospital. I want to take that ambulance and bust out of the gates. I'm fairly sure the guards would let me out, but there's a chance they'll stop me and search the ambulance, standard protocol on a lockdown. *So how did they miss me earlier?* Oh wait, of course they missed me earlier. Earlier, Angela was not on Team Brew. She probably orchestrated the whole thing. The guards were expecting her. It was all part of the ruse. If I'd had my memories, I'd have never fallen for that. Instead I was an eighteen-year-old boy who thought he was in a James Bond movie.

"Doctor Brew, what are we doing here?"

And I realize that I've been lost in my thoughts for a little too long, trying to make this difficult decision.

So I make it. I grab Carrie's arm and take off running towards the admiral's house.

Chapter 37

1550

I'm freezing my buns off right now because I gave Carrie my jacket. Rowing across the Elizabeth River in the dead of winter is a little freaking crazy, but at least we're not swimming. With my training I'm confident I could have made it on my own, but no way Carrie survives that swim. The cold, the distance.

So instead of stealing an ambulance from MediCorp, I stole the next best thing: a canoe from the admiral. They weren't locked. Why would they be? Who would steal a canoe from a two-star admiral? The boat house, a mere thirty yards from the admiral's residence, has been there since the 1930s. It became less useful after the downtown tunnel let cars traverse the water, but it still has boats. It took us a minute to drag the canoe from the shed to the edge of the water. It was challenging getting Carrie in without tipping the damn thing over, but we did it. And now we're halfway across the water, and I'm starting to warm up a bit because this is hard work and I'm rowing fast.

Taking the canoe gives us some distinct advantages. The Chinese consulate is directly across the water from the hospital. No, not *THE* Chinese consulate. The building that the ambassador is staying in. The Norfolk Waterside Hilton. We can actually row right up to the hotel and walk into the lobby in fifteen minutes. At this time of the day, even if the guards somehow let us off base, there's no guarantee tunnel traffic wouldn't have stopped us in our tracks. More opportunities to be nabbed by the agency.

But I'm secretly hoping the ambulance driver and his partner got another call and need to get off base, because Carrie's phone, live SIM card and all, is underneath the driver's seat, and my SIM-less phone is in my pocket. We should be off grid for the moment. My arms are starting to burn and our pace has slowed.

"Doc, I can help. Let me row for a minute, it might help me warm up a little." Carrie's cheeks are deep red and she looks so young and frail right now. But I remember that in high school she rowed crew at Exeter, so she can probably handle this. I hand the oar over and she goes to work. She's remarkably efficient. We're moving a little faster now, her fresh arms propelling us forward. I'm grateful for a chance to call Amy, and find that cell reception isn't as bad as I thought it'd be in the middle of the water.

I skip the pleasantries and get right to the point. "Are you and the girls safe?"

"Yes, Ben, we're safe. I picked everyone up from school early and we're headed back ho—"

"Don't go there, it's not safe," I shout. "Turn around and head to the address I put in your phone."

"Wh—, what address?"

I don't know how secure this line is. I tell Amy to check the glove compartment for a sheet of paper with an address and a code. "Go there, use the code to get in, and wait for me to call you. There's money, food, and clothes for the kids. You should have everything you need for at least a couple of days."

In all honesty, there was everything she needed for an entire month in my DC condo. This is my safe house. I bought it years ago for lying low if things went south—and just like in the movies, it has everything I need: money, fake passports, weapons. It's essentially a huge safe room—Plexiglas windows, titanium-reinforced doors, secure communication capabilities. My family will be safe until I get there. The agency has no idea I have it. I wanted it in Washington, DC, because it's a big city with multiple travel options in case things go really sour. I think it's safe to say things have gone south today. Like deep south. Alabama deep. I'm not sure if it was my wife filleting my ear like a nervous sushi chef or having to choke out my dad WWE-style next to a pool of vomit that clued me in . . .

"You sure are full of surprises, my love. Thanks for keeping us safe," Amy whispers into the phone. No doubt Ana is listening in, wondering why they aren't going home and what Daddy is "keeping us safe" from.

"I love you too, Amy. I promise to meet you all there soon. Don't stop for anything. As soon as you get there, send me a text to let me know you're safe."

I think of one last thing. "And babe, you should probably cancel my birthday party tonight. I'm not sure I can handle any more fun today."

Chapter 38

1613

The lobby of the Waterside Hilton is warm and has complimentary coffee. I am grateful for both. We lounge in some plush red chairs beside a roaring fire and the feeling slowly returns to my face and fingers. Carrie still has my jacket on but her color is better. She and I have a lot to discuss after our relatively silent jaunt across the water.

Her first question catches me off guard. "Why did you leave Angie with those agents? And how did she know so much about the microchip stuff?"

It appears it is time to come clean. Carrie has no idea her best friend is a low-level agent, a plant, but she needs to know the truth. I need her to trust me again. Her life, my life, maybe even Angela's, depend on it.

"Carrie, Angela has been working for the agency for almost two years," I say matter-of-factly. "Your father wanted someone who would be close to you when male Secret Service agents couldn't be. He wanted to make sure you were near someone you could trust and confide in. And Angela, from all my conversations with her, is very much that person. She loves you and values your friendship. Yes, her job is to protect you, but I know that being your friend is more important to her than getting paid to keep you safe."

I'm watching her face. She looks like she's going to cry. She gathers herself and says, "That's really beautiful. I believe you. And I get it, I do. I always wondered why Angela seemed so mature and responsible. Is she really just twenty?"

I smile and nod. "Yes, all the details of her personal life that she's shared with you are true, save her reason for coming to ODU. Trust me, it has pained her to not be completely honest with you. In fact, she's been pushing your dad over the past few months to let her tell you the truth, because she honestly felt that if you knew the truth, it wouldn't change your relationship one bit. It might actually make it easier for her to do her job." I look down into the steaming, black abyss of my coffee cup, hoping my words are comforting but fearing they are simply creating more questions.

Carrie clears her throat. "Ha. Angela knows me well. She's right. I know there were times last year that I tried to hide my drug use from her because I was embarrassed. But she was one of the reasons I stopped. Our friendship is that important to me. But I am going to kick her butt when I see her—she should have told me earlier!"

I'm glad to see this positive response. I need Carrie today as much as she needs me, and now it's much easier for me to ask my first question. "You're sure that the Chinese foreign minister has a chip?"

She stares blankly into the fire as she answers. "Yeah, the foreign minister, the ambassador, and one or two of the consulate generals in the US. I overheard my dad talking about it one night about five months ago in the Oval Office with the director. I was doing my homework after a date with Dad, and the director barged in, worried about some pending diplomatic crisis. They were talking about erasing the memories of specific conversations—so they could try the conversations again with a different approach to get a different outcome.

"It was really hard to not listen; I couldn't believe what I was hearing. Later that night, after the director had left, I asked my dad if those chips were real, and if what he was doing was . . . ethical. We got into a yelling match and he told me to never mention it again." Carrie stands up and walks closer to the fire, seemingly lost in her thoughts. She's got my full attention.

"So I mentioned it again a week later. That conversation went worse than the first one. I didn't mention it again. But it kept bugging me. Several nights, before I went to bed, I rehearsed in my bathroom what I would say to my dad. I even debated telling Angela. But now it makes sense. My memories of those rehearsed conversations were erased right around the time I'd be taking my evening medications. You guys really screwed with my head, you know that?" Now she turns away from the fire to look at me, her eyes alive and awake. "Yeah, I know you're sorry, but aren't you 'adults' supposed to be the responsible ones? I think the only way to get my dad to listen now is to threaten to expose his secret to the Chinese consul general here in Norfolk. I've grown closer to his daughter over the last few months—we've had dinners together, she's in one of my electives. I think her father deserves to know that we can mess with his memory. She's my friend— her father doesn't deserve this."

I don't disagree. The program should have never gone this far. But Carrie has no idea what type of crapocalypse will erupt if the Chinese find out about the microchip. *Did I really just think up the word "crapocalypse?" I must really be trying to clean up my potty mouth.* At the same time, this type of fear should get the president's attention and get him to shut down the program. I need to reassure Carrie that we will make this right—without putting national security at stake.

"Let's call your dad. Tell him where we are. That we're in the lobby of the Norfolk Waterside Hilton with Consul General Wang and his daughter. That unless he immediately shuts down the chips, and sends me verification that it's been done, we'll tell the consul general everything."

Carrie nods her head approvingly and stares off into space, as if watching a movie in her mind of her father accepting our demands. "That should work. He'll be in a corner and forced to do to the right thing. I like this plan. Should we call Consul Wang and Bernice down for a visit? I can make up a story that you're my crew instructor and we fell into the river during practice. I'll tell Bernice that I want her dad to meet my coach, who also happens to be my doctor. You and Angie aren't the only ones who can act . . . "

I smile at Carrie and watch her stride to the concierge desk to call the consul's room. I doubt she'll be given trouble—she is the president's daughter and won't hesitate to remind the staff if she meets any resistance. I check the time on my phone—I still want to get to connect with my contact at the *Virginian Pilot*. A more prestigious newspaper like the *Boston Globe* might be better, but I don't really have that option. Though there's no doubt in my mind that President Banning will agree to our demands, it's always helpful to have a Plan B.

Five minutes later, Consul General Wang and Bernice exit the main elevators. Carrie runs up to Bernice and embraces her. I introduce myself to Wang and thank him for meeting us at such short notice. Carrie casually says she wants to call her dad to let him know she's safe and that she's meeting up with Bernice and her dad. She uses my phone to dial into a secure White House line and turns on the video function.

"Hi, Dad, it's Carrie . . . yeah, I'm fine, I'm safe. I'm standing in the Norfolk Waterside Hilton lobby with Consul General Wang and Bernice. See?" She turns the phone towards the two Chinese nationals and then back to herself. "We were just about to have a little conversation about technology. Can I speak to you in private for one minute?" She takes the phone off of video chat and puts it up to her ear. She turns to face me and whispers into the phone, "Turn them off, Dad. All of them. Or I swear I will tell them the truth. What you're doing is wrong and it needs to stop. Now."

As Carrie listens intently to her dad's response, the lines in her forehead grow deeper. I don't know how to interpret her expression, but then her words do the trick. "No, you listen to me!" she whispers forcefully. Wang and Bernice are amusing themselves, speaking to each other in Mandarin. In another minute or two, this could get pretty awkward. "I understand what's going on and I don't care—you end this program now and prove that you've done it, and we'll say goodbye and walk right out of this hotel."

She turns to flash a fake smile at Bernice and her dad.

And then Wang crumples to the ground, his body writhing. I'm instantly at his side, my advanced cardiac life support training pushing me into action. Bernice is screaming something in Mandarin, and Carrie yells, "What's happening?"

Wang foams at the mouth. I try to use my finger to clear his airway. His eyes roll to the back of his head and his nose begins to bleed. I initiate CPR but one minute into it I know it's no use. Wang is gone.

I stop doing chest compressions and look at Bernice, who is holding her father's head and bawling. I look up at Carrie and she drops my phone. "Is he . . . is he dead? Wh—, what happened?"

And I know exactly what's happened.

Chapter 39

1631

There are only two people in the entire world who know how to turn the MemSave microchip into a weapon of death: me and the director. It was his idea. Once the two of us agreed that implanting chips into super-soldiers was a reasonable idea, it only made sense that if they were captured in combat, one way of protecting them from prolonged torture or divulging key mission details was to either wipe their memory— or mercifully kill them.

But while it was my dad's idea, I was the one who figured out how to implement it. It wasn't truly a kill switch. It was simpler than that. In the lab, when I programmed the chip to overstimulate the hippocampus in mice, the result was hippocampal hemorrhage: essentially inducing a brain stroke. The autopsy on Wang would show that he had a fatal brain hemorrhage, but it'd never discover that a microchip in his ear was the source of it. Ear dissection is not a routine part of a forensic investigation.

I have failed. This is the one outcome I did not anticipate. I'm not worried about myself or Carrie. I deactivated our chips in the mainframe and I have the only password to reactivate them—I think. But instead of meeting our demands, the president opted to end an innocent man's life. Now I know how far he and my father are willing to go to protect this program. I'm wondering why they didn't just bomb the entire hotel and eliminate the biggest threats: me and Carrie. They must still value our lives . . . or at least Carrie's.

It's at that moment that I realize I'm not hearing anything. I see Carrie's lips moving, her face strained, her hand squeezing my cell phone like a soaked sponge.

Then my hearing comes back and all hell breaks loose.

Chapter 40

1632

My ears explode with sound, and I squint as pain rips through my head; it feels like a bag of fireworks went off two feet away from me. I hear Carrie loud and clear. "—tor Brew! They're here! Run!"

I swivel around to see four Gs clad in black rushing through the hotel's front door. *Good for you, Dad—you sent more men this time.* I make two calculated decisions at this point.

Calculation #1: They will not shoot live rounds at the president's daughter. I leap to my feet, grab Carrie's arm, and sprint in the opposite direction.

Calculation #2: Our only leverage is dead, so our only chance—my only chance—to survive is to get this information to the press, to the *Virginian Pilot.* We must escape by any means necessary.

I pull Carrie towards the escalators and sprint up two stairs at a time. Agents are yelling "Get down," and though the lobby isn't busy, the guests present for this spectacle begin to freak out. After all, the Gs are holding very large guns and yelling. We knock over a middle-aged man on the way up the escalator and find ourselves on the mezzanine.

I see a stairwell at the end of the mezzanine. Two of the four Gs are already halfway up the escalator. We run towards the stairs and I slam the metal door open. "Carrie, run up to the third floor and I'll meet you by the elevators. Go!" I can tell she doesn't want to leave me but there's no time to explain. The two Gs are ten yards from the stairwell as I let the door slowly close. I don't see them, but I know because it only took me thirty strides to reach this spot and I can hear them approaching. The one in front has a slight limp, and I'm pretty sure it's the guy Angela dealt with less than kindly at Chang's place earlier. Agency must be short-staffed today. I'm sure Holley wants payback.

I hear Carrie reach the third-floor deck and open the creaky door. Good. I didn't think she had the stamina to make it much higher, and the third floor is important if the rest of this patchwork plan is going to work. I'm still holding the handle with my left hand, so the door is three feet ajar and my back's against the door.

I use psychology often in moments of conflict. A door that was slammed open seconds earlier isn't moving, so the expectation is that it's stuck. You expect the people you're chasing to go up or down the staircase because they are running away from you. You don't expect one of them to be waiting behind the door, waiting to slam it with the full force of his body into your own.

But that's what happens. I've timed it perfectly. The second I hear the lead agent's foot smack the concrete floor of the stairwell, I launch my shoulder into the door. I feel the crunch as his body is sandwiched

161

between the door and the metal frame. He grunts and I suspect two or three rib fractures. I yank the door open and plant my right elbow into his left flank with a satisfying crack that doubles him over. My right knee meets his jaw and I thrust him into the arms of his partner, who's trailing him by only a few feet.

I jump forward, grabbing the doorframe, swinging my legs up and twisting my hips clockwise. My double kick meets his nose and sternum simultaneously. He crumples to the ground moaning and I land on my feet in the ready position, expecting to see the other two agents . . . but I don't. I turn around and sprint up to the third floor, throwing the door open and finding myself in the hallway. I see Carrie at the end of the hall, about thirty yards away. She starts to jog towards me. As I jog towards her, the elevator opens behind her.

Two agents.

"Run!" I yell, closing the gap between us in seconds. The agents are close. I grab Carrie and shove her past a room-service cart into an open room. I slam the door behind me. The housekeeping lady clutches a pillow to her chest as I pull Carrie to the balcony, throw the curtains aside, and slide the door open. I step out into the cold air and look down.

Damn. There's a pool, but we'd need to be on the balcony of Room 324 to jump into it. This was not part of the plan. *Jumping into the pool from the third floor: the stuff of movies. What was I thinking? Maybe I'm thinking I'm eighteen again?* The sound of the agents slamming into the door momentarily breaks my attention. I rub my forehead and close my eyes. *Think, Brew. There is a way out of this.* I open my eyes and turn around. Carrie is tying sheets end to end. The maid is helping her.

I love this girl. I take over the knot-tying and tell her to tell the agents to step away and that she will walk out. I know they won't discharge their weapons into the door.

"You have ten seconds, Ms. Banning, and then we will forcibly come in," an agent shouts.

I tie one end of the rope to the balcony rail and tug on it to test it. It's not going to be quite long enough, and she'll have to let go about seven feet from the ground. I gesture for Carrie to come over to me.

"Carrie, once you're down, you need to go directly to the *Virginian Pilot* and find Bill Simons."

"You're not coming with me?" She's terrified.

I grasp her by the shoulders, much like I did with Amy back at the house. "There's not time. Tell Bill you want someone from the legal department present—and then tell him everything you know. Then c—"

"Call my dad and tell him that if anything happens to me, you, or Angela, and if the chip program isn't immediately halted, I'll release the info."

I nod.

"You have three seconds!" the agent yells. I give Carrie a hug and help her over the balcony rail, lowering her down slowly. She's a good kid. A smart kid. I don't doubt she'll be successful. I just hope I can st—

"Step away from the door!" Two seconds later, gunfire erupts. I assume they've shot the hinges. The maid sits on the bed on her knees, her hands interlocked over her head. She's sobbing loudly. I am in the middle of the room, on my knees, head bowed, my hands behind my head.

The agents burst into the room, guns drawn.

"Where is she?" the lead agent yells. I look up at him and smile. The other one checks the bathroom, the closet. He looks under the bed while his partner keeps his gun trained on my chest.

The lead agent unlocks the balcony door and walks out onto it. In a handful of seconds, he'll see the patch of sheets on the grass below and realize Carrie is gone. I laugh out loud, not intending to sound sinister, but I surprise myself. *I have an evil laugh . . .*

"She's gone," he yells over my laughter. He takes two steps towards me and places the gun on my forehead. He repeats himself slowly, seething. He's failed his mission, and his boss—my dad—won't be happy.

"Where . . . is . . . she?"

I smile at him and reply just as slowly, "For . . . POTUS's . . . ears . . . only."

He backs away, gun still trained on me, and pulls his cell from his pocket to answer it in a hushed whisper. I make out quite a few "no" answers and stick out my bottom lip mockingly while gently shaking my head.

I take a moment to bask in my success. My father is probably on the other end of the line, frustrated. I am still at least one step ahead of him. He may anticipate my next play, but Carrie has hopefully already caught a cab to the newspaper and has a good head start. I do wonder how the agents were able to find us at the hotel so quickly. We had no tracking devices. They couldn't have gotten to our location that quickly even when we did explicitly give them our location on the phone call to POTUS. The only other person who knew where we were going . . .

Shit.

Angela.

And then the agent takes two steps towards me and all I see is the barrel of his gun coming at my face before the room goes dark.

Chapter 41

1644

For the second time today, I wake up with a splitting headache. But I'm not in my memory-foam bed with the down comforter. Amy's not beside me.

No, wherever I am now smells like gym socks and sweat. And it's cold. My shirt is off. *Dang it, I really liked that shirt.*

I must be blindfolded because I can't see a darn thing.

"Hey, I think he's coming around." I recognize the voice of the agent that knocked me out. Still feeling woozy, I try to get my bearings.

My hands are tied together with a zip tie, and they're attached to something above my head, though I'm in a sitting position. I lean back and feel cold, unforgiving metal. Every tiny movement I make seems to echo, like I'm the last chocolate chip cookie in Grandpa's Christmas tin. Mmmm...cookies sound good right now. Unfortunately, no amount of positive thinking is going to change the fact that I'm probably in the back of an agency van.

But I'm not alone. I smell something familiar (not cookies). No, *someone* familiar (not Grandpa).

Angela.

I can't believe she's still working with them after all we've been through. She is the only one who could have led them to the hotel. But she's young, so I get it. Maybe they made her an offer she couldn't refuse? I mean, what could they have offered her to make her betray—

No . . . they wouldn't . . . but they would.

"Angela?" I ask weakly. I really wish I could see right now.

"Hey, Brew . . . I . . . I really tried to hold out as long as I could. But . . . but it hurt so bad. I'm so sorry." She sniffles and I can tell she is hurt, emotionally and physically. I feel ashamed for entertaining the idea that she'd ratted us out. She would never have given up our location unless she was coerced. She never had the training I had. She never underwent torture training, save for the most basic captivity training that every agent and soldier receives. And if they threatened her family, how could she resist? I'm angry with myself for thinking a nineteen-year-old college student would be able to stand up to two seasoned Secret Service agents. I'm sure my father was behind this as well, and I'm determined to make them pay for what they've done to her.

"I know, I can't look me in the eye either right now, Brew. Not my proudest moment."

Does she think I can see her? I'm blindfolded. And it's a good blindfold because it's dark as hell in this va—but why don't I feel the blindfold on my face? I'm blinking and I don't feel the cloth on my eyelashes . . .

For the love of God. Of all times to get the blindness side effect of my chip. This is rich. It feels so absurd that I want to laugh out loud, but I can't let Angela or the agents know. Right now, I'm smarter than everyone in the back of this van, which is why Angela and I are going to make it out of here alive, but I need to know what I'm working with.

"How many of them did it take to drag you in here? I'm guessing six," I say, my face tilted towards Angela's voice. I'm hoping she'll play along.

"Nah, apparently only takes two grown-ass men to beat up one young female. If it had been these two guys, I might have fared better."

Nice, Angela, just what I needed. I'm guessing it's just the two agents I confronted in the hotel room. I was sort of hoping for the two beat-up ones I left on the mezzanine—or Jim and Terry so I could exact full revenge. Oh well, someone will be punished. The agents in the back of the van with us make disapproving noises, so I know where they are. Agent #1 is directly across from me, to the left of Angela. Agent #2 is about three feet to my left. I hear Agent #1 on his phone and recognize his voice. He's saying "Yes, sir" repeatedly. He seems to pause during his phone call to address me.

"This is your last chance to tell us where the president's daughter is."

"Or you'll knock me out with your gun again? That was so helpful last time."

He resumes his phone conversation. "He's not telling us anything. We'll start heading back to the agency . . . Yes, sir."

I hear Agent #2 get up from his spot beside me and move towards the front of the van, keys jingling. I assume Angela is restrained in the same fashion I am. But now we have the advantage. Sort of. The van rumbles to life and we begin to move. I settle my mind and try to pay attention to our location, my mental map charting our path. *Right onto St. Paul's. Left on Church Street. Slight left onto 460 as it turns into Gran—*

Agent #1 can't keep his pie hole shut. "I need to get you back to HQ in one piece, so the director's authorized me to start beating up your little girlfriend here unless you start talking. She looks like she could use another good beating," he says while chuckling and cracking his knuckles. "How many fingers does a pretty girl really need?"

I am going to hurt this agent badly. But he's already given me power over him—I know that no matter what I do, he won't use lethal force against me.

I feel the van rising, which tells me, even though I'm as blind as a bat, that Agent #2 is merging the van onto the onramp for I-64. That means in one minute we'll be on the Hampton Roads Bridge. That's where I'll make my move.

But I need to stall. I can't take a chance that he'll hurt Angela. "Ok, ok," I begin meekly, "please don't hurt her. I'll tell you . . . what you need to know. But I . . . I really need my medicine." I cough forcefully. My shoulders are beginning to dull from the pain of having my hands strung up above my head. I groan and struggle against the zip tie.

"What medicine? C'mon, tough guy. Just tell us where Carrie is. We'll be at the agency in twenty minutes and we can take you to medical. This isn't a waaah-mbulance."

Agent #2 chuckles from the front. "Oooh, burn."

"No!" I bellow. "I need my medicine now! If I don't get it soon . . . my . . . my heart." I groan even louder, and my right leg starts to twitch. I feel a bump as the van climbs onto the bridge and begins its ascent. Now is the time.

"Just calm down," the agent tells me, his voice belying his concern. "Larry, step on the gas, we need to get to HQ pronto!"

My plan is working. Since I was six years old and rode my first bus to school, I've had a penchant for car sickness. Usually buses and vans, and almost always on bridges. Over the years I've learned to control the nausea, mind over matter. But today I'm going to let matter take over.

And that's when I begin to vomit all over myself.

Chapter 42

1650

As I vomit, I dissociate from the experience and lock myself in my mind and spirit, hoping for a brief moment of meaningful reflection. Without my vision, I'm not sure how to execute this plan to perfection.

I feel like Samson, the Biblical judge who derived supernatural strength from his hair. But I'm not feeling supernaturally strong or like I'm in a position to kick anyone's butt with the jawbone of an ass. I feel like end-of-the-road Samson, post-Delilah-betrayal. Strength gone, tied up in the pagan temple, the laughing stock of the enemy. My dad has betrayed me but I've betrayed my friends, my soldiers, and then some. I feel weak, I'm strung up in the back of a van, covered in my own vomit, and these agents are making a mockery of my captivity. So, like Samson, I ask God for one more chance. One more chance to prove myself. To right my wrongs. I ask for clarity of vision—both physically and spiritually. Somehow, over the course of the last few years, I lost my way. I ask for forgiveness as I continue to heave, and it's as if a great weight is leaving me, the filth within me being purged, and with each deep breath, new life flows inward. I remember words from a Bible passage: *My power is made perfect in weakness.*

And my vision returns.

I survey the scene. It's not pretty. There's vomit everywhere, in front me, on my pants and shoes, Angela is beginning to dry heave, and Agent #1 stands directly in front of me, gun in hand, his face contorted in a grimace. My advantage grows stronger. *Power is made perfect in weakness.* I can't look any weaker to Agent #1. I'm vomiting and crying. He thinks I could be having a medical emergency. He believes I am vulnerable.

I have never been more dangerous.

"Lay me flat! Lay me flat!" I cry, and he rushes to my side, holsters his gun, and pulls out his field knife, cutting my bonds with a decisive flick of his wrist. I crumple into the pile of my own vomit because I need a few seconds for the blood to rush back into my arms and hands. I continue to writhe but I'm done vomiting. Mind resumes its rightful place over matter, even though we're still on the bridge.

Most nonmedical personnel don't do very well with bodily fluids. Blood's usually no big deal for a well-trained agent, but feces, urine, and vomit? There's no training for that in the field guide. Even after eighteen years of medical experience, I'd be lying if I said lying in vomit was easy, but I've handled worse. Agent #1 hasn't.

"Faster, Larry!" I can feel Agent #1 standing over me. He tugs at my shoulder in an attempt to flip me over and see my face. I assume this means he's sheathed his knife. I'm about to do something I've never done before, but since this has been a day of firsts, it's really not that remarkable. I make myself feel like dead weight, the way my kids feel when I'm carrying them upstairs to put them to bed after a long night out—except that they're actually awake and pretending to be asleep. Now I feel both of his hands on me, one on my right shoulder, one on my hip. He's definitely not holding a knife. As he turns me on my side, I grab a fistful of vomit and fling it in his face.

He recoils and I lash out with my right leg, kicking the outside of his left knee. I feel a snap as my own leg locks—but it's not my knee snapping. It's his. I've either torn or severely sprained his medial collateral ligament. He drops to that knee but he's recovering from my vomit faster than anticipated. Instinct prevails, I guess—he'd managed to unholster his Beretta while barf-blinded, and the barrel is rising towards my fa—

Angela kicks her left leg straight up. A bullet whizzes past by head. It may have grazed me, because I feel the burn of the gun's discharge against my cheek and am temporarily disoriented by the light and sound. But I don't have time to process the fact that my life just flashed before my eyes, because the agent is already lowering his gun for a second shot. The van lurches to the right and my body slams into the wall. The sound of grating metal fills the cabin. I catch a glimpse of Larry slumped over the wheel clutching his neck as blood spurts through his fingers.

Holey severed carotid, this is not g—

And then my body levitates and slams into the roof of the van, because we're falling into the James River.

Chapter 43

1659

One of my earliest memories is of being three years old and taking swimming lessons at the YMCA in Minneapolis. The pool smelled like a delightful concoction of toe jam and chlorine. The other kids were about my age but a little bigger than me. I was puny, my West African genetics dooming me to a lifetime of short stature.. My dad grew up fishing and swimming on the coast of Ghana, and it was important that his sons know how to swim.

But I hated swimming. I was terrified of the water, and the foam-tablet life jacket strapped to my chest and back gave me little comfort. So imagine my displeasure when they told us it was time to swim without our flotation devices. We all lined up at the edge of the pool waiting our turn.

And then the details become murky. Did the teacher tell me to jump in and swim to her? Or was I just standing too close to the edge and I slipped in? Regardless, I remember sinking straight to the bottom of the pool. But that wasn't the most terrifying part of the memory. It was the fact that the pool was maybe only three feet deep. And I wasn't three feet tall. I could see adult-sized shapes moving above the water, but none of them were moving towards me. I felt like I was under the water for an eternity. I felt helpless.

And then someone pulled me out of the water, and I remember gasping for air, crying, and knowing that I never wanted to feel that way again. You would have thought that over the course of my childhood, I would have committed myself to becoming a world-class swimmer. You would have thought wrong. Yeah, I became a decent swimmer. We had a backyard pool once we moved to Texas. I honed my swimming skills during the summer but never took formal lessons again. What I really worked on, probably weekly, over all those years? Holding my breath. Keeping perfectly still in water, I can hold my breath for nearly three minutes.

When the airborne van finally hits the water, I've curled my body into a tight ball, my head tucked in, knees clutched tightly to my chest, bracing for impact. I strike the windshield like a cannonball—thankfully with my feet and butt and not my head. Being in a government van is somewhat beneficial in this instance. In a normal car, I would have shattered the windshield and water would be gushing in at the moment. As it turns out, only Larry's window was open. Maybe he rolled it down to allow the smell of my vomit to escape . . . before he was hit by a wayward bullet. My guess is he doesn't survive this ordeal; his open window gift to us lowers our chances as well.

As I lie in brackish water, I momentarily try to ignore the pain shooting through my lower legs and back. I don't think the drop off the bridge was more than thirty feet, but I'm hurt. Hopefully being tied in has protected

Angela to a certain extent. She is my only priority. I feel the weight of Agent #1's torso on me. As I push him off, I notice his neck is twisted in an unnatural position. I pull the knife out of his leg sheath. He won't be needing it anymore.

Water is filling the van and it's surreal watching the bottom of the river approach slowly through the windshield. I don't have a lot of time. Angela is moaning as I crawl up towards her and the weight of the van's engine pulls us downward. We hit the bottom and I briefly lose my grip, dropping into the pool that has formed in the front cabin of the van. I grab the back of the passenger's seat and haul myself up. Angela's feet are now only inches from my face. The van has leveled out a little and I'm able to walk—no, wade—to Angela's position. I'm about to cut Angela free when I realize it'll be tough to get a semiconscious woman out of a water coffin. The van continues to fill and I feel the water reach my knees, which surprisingly still work. I grab Angela's head and try to coax her to wake up. Seconds later, her eyes open.

"That bit with the vomit was pretty nasty," her voice finding a higher pitch on the last two words. "Please tell me you've washed your hands."

I laugh and reach up to cut her hands free. She slumps to the floor and I grab her under the arms to keep her from sliding into the water. She immediately clutches her side and pulls up her shirt to reveal a heavily bruised torso. I suspect internal injuries; I need to get her to a hospital quickly. Rather than wait for the van to completely fill with water, I tell her that if she's able, we should swim down to the open driver's window and out of the van.

"I don't think I can do it, Brew. I'm . . . I'm broken." And then I remember her injuries from earlier in the day. She needs me more than ever. I tell her I only need her help getting through the window and then I'll do the rest. She doesn't look convinced.

"Can I ask you a question, Ben? It's one I've been dying to ask for the last few hours," she says, reaching up to touch her ear.

"Sure, sweetie. I'm all ears." The words slip out before I realize how silly I sound.

"I know I have a chip. I suspect you or the president had it placed. What did you erase? If I'm going to die today, I'd like to at least know what I'm forgetting."

The water is up to our waists as we stand on the bench. In thirty seconds, it will be up to our necks.

I remember clearly the one and only time I wiped Angela's memory. It will be more painful for her to relive than me. I even debated wiping the memory at all. There's a good chance she wouldn't have remembered the event anyway, given her mental state that night. I decide to tell her, because there's a good chance that neither of us will survive this day. And she has a right to know.

"About six months ago, you drunk-dialed me after a night of partying with Carrie. You said that you really needed to see me. I could tell you were drunk but you said it was extremely important. I showed up to Carrie's dorm room around one A.M. She was already asleep when I walked into the room; the door was cracked open." This is where I pause, unsure if I should continue, but I do. "As soon as I walked in, you jumped me—literally. I caught you in my arms and you wrapped your legs around my waist. And then you . . . you st—"

"I started kissing you, and despite you trying to push me away, I kept coming at you. I professed my love for you. I told you that your wife was a lucky woman, and then I suggested some inappropriate adult activities for us to indulge in. Yeah, now I remember." My arms are still wrapped around her waist and our faces are inches apart. I'm not sure which one of us feels more embarrassed right now.

"Angela, I just thought that night would change our relationship forever. It would have been almost impossible to work closely together. The tension would have killed our ability to keep Carrie safe." The water is up to our necks. "You're beautiful," I tell her, looking directly into her pale green eyes. "And in another life, under different circumstances, I would be yours, and you would be mine. You're a keeper. But in this life, I'm married to the woman of my dreams . . . and I have kids . . . and I'm one of your bosses. I love you dearly, and that's why there's no more time to talk. Because at this rate, your future husband will never get to meet you and I'm not ok with that."

I kiss her on the forehead and hold her close, speaking quietly. "We're about to go under. I need you to hyperventilate for fifteen seconds and then take a deep breath. Ok?" Her cheek is warm against mine as she whispers back, teeth chattering. And as the water reaches our chin, Angela takes my face in her wet hands and kisses me on my lips before I can protest.

"Thank you. I love you, Benjamin Brew." And in that "thank you," that "I love you," I think she understands why I did what I did. I could have gotten her fired, especially if I had reported her drunkenness while on duty and her behavior towards me. I don't think erasing that memory changed her feelings for me—but I think it preserved our working relationship, and I knew what boundaries to keep between us. Angela now understood the distance I had been keeping with her over the last few months. But today, in this very moment, we had never been closer.

She pulls me closer one more time, her arms wrapped around my shoulder. I feel her warm breath on my ear as she begins to hyperventilate. No doubt there is some fear spurring her on; she's not just following my orders. I can feel her belly pressing rhythmically against mine. I begin to hyperventilate with her, adrenaline coursing through my veins as I execute the trick I learned back in medical school for increasing oxygen-carrying capacity while breath-holding. Angela's breath abruptly changes as she takes in a prolonged, deep breath.

And then we go under.

Chapter 44

1703

One minute and seventeen seconds.

That's my calculation of how long I'll need to hold my breath to break the surface with Angela in tow.

Unfortunately, based on her profound anemia, as presented in the paleness of her skin and oral mucosa, bruised or broken ribs, unknown internal injuries, and multiple leg contusions—Angela will only have fifty-eight seconds.

That's a lot of time to not be oxygenating.

It only takes us seven or eight seconds to get down to the driver's-side window. I didn't anticipate how much the bodies at the front of the van would move while we were planning our escape. Larry's body drifts in front of the window in a cloudy pool of his own blood. Poor SOB...poor shortness of breath! *I have no idea why I'm cracking medical/expletive jokes at a time like this, but didn't I say something earlier about humor and fear?* As I swim down, pulling Angela with me, I take a quick glance up and see there's no time to swim back up for another breath after moving Larry's body. Angela holds onto the steering wheel during the ten seconds it takes me to make space for her to swim through. This is extra energy and time I hadn't accounted for. I push her through the window with one hand, pulling Larry out of the way with the other. Before she's fully through I begin to launch myself forward—but my foot gets caught. I wriggle my leg but it seems to be caught between Larry and the window frame. I push on his body but can't wiggle free. I look through the murky water above me and see Angela very slowly making her way to the surface, which seems a lot farther away than I anticipated. There is no way she is going to make it. It's been thirty-five seconds now and with all the energy I've expended, I'm beginning to panic. I reach for the knife stashed in my belt because I realize it's not Larry that's caught me but his seatbelt. I cut it and five seconds later I'm free. My chest is burning and I've lost track of time. I push off as hard as I can from the van door. I'm kicking as hard as I can, and I am almost to Angela's feet. She's not moving very well.

I have a decision to make. At my current speed, I should make it to the top in eleven seconds. If I stop and pull Angela with me, neither of us will make it.

I make the obvious choice but there's no way to tell Angela. I swim by her and catch a glimpse of her face. I can't tell if it's hate or disappointment. But as soon as I'm by her, I see her quit trying to swim, and she opens her mouth, bubbles escaping, as if to say goodbye. But it's the look on her face that really gets me—the same face she made when telling me the story of her dad's death, how she felt abandoned. I want to cry out to her, tell her how much I care for her, tell her how sorry I am for everything that has happened today. But I just keep swimming. Only five more seconds until I reach the surface. I feel myself passing out.

I release the tiny pocket of air in my mouth but I'm not yet to the surface. Black patches pepper my vision. My arms feel like lead, my legs are barely churning. Just two more strokes and . . .

I break the surface and inhale deeply, and without missing a beat, I dive back down to save the girl that loves me.

Chapter 45

1705

The frigid water would bother me more if I wasn't doing so much work. It's one thing keeping my own head above the water. It's another thing keeping Angela's as I swim on my back towards shore, Angela's lifeless body pinned against my chest, my hands clasped tightly around her sternum. I squeeze her rhythmically against my body as I kick, singing the Bee Gees' "Staying Alive" in my head. If I survive this day, I'll patent my CPR-while-swimming technique. The whole purpose of CPR is to keep the heart pumping, which keeps blood flowing to the brain and other vital parts of the body. I have no idea whether or not Angela has a heartbeat. Thankfully when I swam back down to get her, she wasn't too far down, but she spent at least twelve seconds passed out underwater.

One hundred meters later, I've reached shore. I drag her onto dry ground and collapse with her head on my stomach. I reach deep inside myself and find the strength to sit up and begin chest compressions, followed by two mouth-to-mouth breaths. I start another round of compressions. With the next mouth breaths, she sputters to life, spitting water into my face and rolling onto her side. She's laboring but she's breathing. I'm crouched over her, waiting to do a full medical assessment but just happy that she's alive. She rolls onto her back and looks me in the eye.

"Now I know what to do to get some attention from you, Brew." I smile and brush the wet hair out of her face. "When you swam by me, for a brief second, I thought you had left me. My last, gargled words were going to be 'Benjamin Brew, you son of a b— aaarrrghh.'" She does an excellent job simulating drowning noises for someone who just nearly drowned. "But I didn't want to waste my final breath on your punkass if I was going out like that. I held on for another few seconds, and as I let my breath go, and my eyes burned holes into your butt, I saw you dive back down. And that's the last thing I remember. So I guess we're even now. That agent would have shot you in the head had I not been quick with my feet." She winks at me, shivering.

"Um, if you hadn't kicked his leg, he wouldn't have shot his partner in the neck . . . you know, that poor son of a gun that drove the van into the river? And then I wouldn't have had to save *you*. I'm pretty sure I would have dodged that first bullet." She rolls her eyes. "The Matrix? I know you were amongst the unborn when that movie came out, but c'mon?" *Not impressed* face persists. "Bullet time aside, who can shoot accurately with vomit in their eyes?" I shrug, resigned to lose this argument of who owes who.

"Oh geez, I almost forgot," she says, sticking her tongue out in disgust. "Please tell me you brushed your teeth between that moment and giving me CPR."

"Should have asked me that before you ambush-kissed me in the van at the bottom of the river." It's too cold to tell if she's blushing. I offer her my hand and pull her into a sitting position. She groans and grimaces and my heart floods with guilt for the pain I've caused her, both physical and emotional. I hear sirens on the bridge and look over. Bystanders are pointing over the water and in our general direction. I wave to make sure they see us. It's time for me to go.

I kneel over her and whisper, "Wait here for EMS," looking warmly and deeply into her sunken eyes. "Get fixed up. I'll catch up with you soon, ok?"

I tell her the address of my safe house and how to contact Amy. I warn her not to spend more than an hour and a half in the hospital, to demand an MRI immediately—doctor's orders—and to get out before the agency finds her. With that, I give her one last delicate hug and jog off into the woods.

Chapter 46

1720

The half-mile hike feels like a half marathon. I'm bare-chested and barefoot and it's early winter in Virginia. But I finally see a house up ahead. Except that it looks more like a palace than a house, and that's just from the back. There's at least three stories and three separate wings. The Olympic-size pool in the backyard has a diving board and a thirty-foot waterslide. I ask myself why I didn't go into plastic surgery. There's no fence, of course, because the owners didn't anticipate a waterside breach of their property. I walk carefully around the pool, scanning the windows for movement. When I reach the covered patio's glass doors, I peer in. All clear.

I whisper a prayer and turn the handle. The door opens soundlessly and I'm in. I walk straight through the covered patio and into the den. Marble flooring. Decorations like pictures I've seen of the Versailles Palace in France. I don't have time to ogle so I take my first left, which brings me straight into the kitchen. The refrigerator is calling my name. I open the stainless steel doors and pull out an ice cold Fiji. It could have been lukewarm toilet water. I down it in seconds. I grab another bottle and close the fridge. And as the door swings shut, in my periphery I see someone staring at me from five feet away. I turn my head slowly.

"Hi, I'm Dr. Brew." It's the first thing that comes to mind. Maybe because it's one of the first things I say when I meet an adolescent in my clinic. Maybe it's because I know I need to put this fourteen-year-old-looking boy of Indian descent at ease. Maybe it's because I know that right now I look nothing like a doctor, so honesty might be the only thing that keeps him from freaking out.

"What kind of doctor are you?" he asks. Hmm, the response I was hoping for but not expecting.

"Pediatrician. Adolescent and young adult medicine, to be specific. I've been in an accident—my car went off that bridge behind your house and I swam to shore. I hope you don't mind that I let myself in. I'm on official government business. I need to make a few phone calls, borrow some clothes from your dad, and maybe even some transportation. I know this sounds outlandish, but you look like a smart kid. There's no reason I'd make any of this up. Google me on your phone there to confirm my identity. While you're doing that, I'm going to head up to your dad's room for some clothes. Which stairwell should I use?"

He points to the west side of the house without batting an eye. Either I'm incredibly persuasive or he's too shocked to do anything but cooperate. Probably a combination of the two. I take off jogging and find the master bedroom after a couple of minutes. There are a lot of doors to check. His father happens to be about my size. A doctor, if I have to guess from the clothes in the massive walk-in closet. I pick something casual and loose-fitting—beige cargo pants, a black turtleneck (who still wears turtlenecks?), and an NYU hoodie. In the master bathroom, I relieve myself and take a good look in the mirror as I wash my hands. I've looked sexier. I clean the dirt and blood from my face and look at myself again. Better. I look around the sink and bypass the blue toothbrush, instead taking a long, burning swig of mouthwash—because using someone else's toothbrush after the places my mouth has been today would be, well, rude.

The tennis shoes I find are a size too small, but they'll have to do. I lost my socks and shoes at the bottom of the river. I jog back down the stairs. The teenager is waiting for me in the lobby. Wow, his house has a lobby.

"Dr. Brew, I really can't let you take my dad's Bentley—it's his baby. But you can take my VW."

This kid is a godsend. "What's your name, son?"

"Nipun, sir. Do you need to use my phone before you leave?" he asks before he hands me a key.

I take his phone and call Amy. She's halfway to DC. I tell her that Angela may show up tonight. She tells me to stay safe and I tell her the same. We exchange I love yous. I open the web browser and look up the *Virginian Pilot* office on Google Maps, memorize the address, and call the main number. I'm finally patched into Bill Simons's office.

"Bill? This is Benjamin Brew."

"Benjamin!" He sounds panicked. "Are you in the lobby?"

"No, Bill, I'm about a twenty-minute drive away. What's wrong?"

"Carrie Banning is lying on the floor in front me, and she's been seizing for ten minutes!"

Chapter 47

1729

Medical residency sucks. The pay is barely minimum wage, which the powers that be justify by saying your future "earning potential" is so great. The work week is eighty to a hundred hours long. There's little time to exercise and the sleep deprivation is constant. On call, in the middle of the night, attendings and nurses expect residents to operate at full capacity. Heck, residents are expected to save lives. Children's lives actually depend on a resident's ability to function on little sleep. A very scary reality.

One of my favorite teachers in residency was Dr. Frank Jones, a pediatric neurologist. I remember how embarrassed I was one night when I paged him frantically when one of his patients began to seize.

"Is she breathing, Benjamin?"

"Yessir!" I yelled into the phone.

"Has she been seizing for more than five minutes?"

"Uh, I think it's been like seven or eight, sir." A nurse tapped my shoulder and corrected me. Two minutes and fifteen seconds, to be exact.

I conveyed the accurate time to Dr. Jones. He patiently taught me two things.

One: A seizing patient is not likely to die. Do not run to their room. Calmly walk when you're notified by the nurse, assess the patient's airway, and prepare to abort the seizure if it lasts for more than five minutes.

Two: Check your pulse. Then check your watch. Seizures always seem to last longer than they actually do, especially to parents and new doctors in training. Seizures look scary. The kid is freaking out, his arms and legs flapping uncontrollably, drool oozing from his mouth, no response to external stimuli. The good thing about a seizure? It will probably stop on its own.

So I don't freak out when I hear Bill Simons's assessment. He hasn't had 12,000+ hours of hands-on medical training. I know Carrie has epilepsy and Bill probably doesn't—I'm not sure he could even spell "epileptiform" seizure. I know Carrie probably missed her 1600 dose. I'm surprised that she's seizing after just one missed dose but it's been a stressful day and I suspect—actually I know—she's missed several doses over the last few weeks because we've tampered with her memories so much. I suspect this seizure has only been about four minutes long, and that any minute now she will stop and enter a post-ictal state—where the brain is pooped out and trying to recover from firing like crazy over the last few minutes. Carrie will probably just lie there with a glazed look on her face for about thirty minutes and then be relatively back to her normal self, except for a wicked headache.

I reassure Bill that Carrie will be fine and tell him which precautions to take. By his description, it sounds like she's already stopped seizing and is in her post-ictal. Because she was so out of it, he assumed she was still seizing.

"Just let her lay still for a little longer. You've probably already called EMS. Please don't let them take her. Tell them her personal doctor is on the way. I don't want them moving her."

Bill's nervous about telling medical personnel what to do, but understands why I'm being so cautious. Carrie is probably safer at the *Virginian Pilot* than anywhere else right now. I ask him to tell me a little bit about what happened before she seized. I'm not sure how much he actually knows.

"She showed up about an hour ago. I put her in the conference room with one of our lawyers. She tells me she's got an explosive story but refuses to share the details with me because her life—and yours—are in danger. So she starts writing a sealed statement and then about five minutes into it, flops to the floor and starts writhing around. What's this all about, Ben? I can help you if I have more information."

"Good try, Bill. That's why I told Carrie to go directly to you. Because you're not terribly persuasive. I'll be there in twenty minutes. If you have any journalistic integrity, do not try to interview her while she's recovering from her seizure." I hear a low growl and then the line goes dead. I think I've made my point.

Nipun has heard this entire conversation so I'm convinced he knows I'm not bullshitting. He enthusiastically shows me to the garage. I instruct him to add my home address and cell to his phone contacts and to have his dad bring him to pick his car up at the *Virginian Pilot* in two hours. I tell him if he needs a recommendation for Harvard or Yale, I'll write him the best damn letter a student's ever received. He beams and waves at me as I pull out of his driveway.

As I merge onto the highway, my mind is running in a million directions. Did they get Angela safely to a hospital? How much did Carrie write before she seized? Bill dare not read it. Would it be enough to frighten her father into reversing course? The very fact that she made it to the newspaper's office is a success. Now I just need to contact the president and the director and let them know where we are. That should get their collective panties in a bundle.

Chapter 48

1746

I surprise myself and pull into a parking space in front of the *Virginian Pilot* in seventeen minutes. Yes, I violated multiple laws while driving. Put it on my tab.

I get out of the car and place the key on top of the front left tire, out of sight. I scan my surroundings and note the ambulance parked in the fire lane twenty yards ahead of me. *Phew, this means Carrie is still in the building*. I sprint up the stairs to the third floor where Bill's office is.

He sees me as I round the corner.

"I couldn't stop them, Ben. They were insistent that she come with them. She was even alert enough to protest but they st—"

I'm already back in the stairwell, taking the stairs three at a time. I'm almost to the first floor when it finally clicks.

The ambulance in the fire lane? Very few markings. Not one of the local transport companies I'm aware of. That wasn't a real ambulance. It's a painted agency van, just like the one I was in forty-five minutes ago.

I should have known the agency was scanning the airwaves for her name, hoping to get a hit. Bill would have used her real name. Probably hadn't thought twice about it.

The agents in the ambulance probably didn't recognize me with the hoodie pulled tightly over my head. If I can make it to the elevator . . .

I sprint through the stairwell door and scan the lobby. No gurney. I abruptly swivel towards the musical ding of the elevator reaching the ground floor, and I break into a full sprint. As the elevator doors open, I lithely jump directly onto the gurney, narrowly avoiding Carrie's prone body. I launch myself at the surprised agents on each side, grabbing a fistful of each agent's jacket. I kick backwards and send the gurney flying into the hallway, propelling myself, agents in hand, into the elevator's back wall with a thud. I land on my feet and punch the one on my left with a hard right, then level a spinning roundhouse with my left foot into the face of the other. I calmly push the button for Floor 12 on my way out of the elevator and adjust my hoodie strings.

Carrie sits up on her elbows, her hair a whirling mess, and flashes a crooked smile. "What's up, Doc?"

Chapter 49

1750

We find a back door and walk briskly down the alley between the newspaper and the AT&T building. To be fair, it feels more like a three-legged race, and my two legs are doing most of the work.

"Now what, genius?" Carrie slurs. She's feisty when she's recovering from a seizure. Her left arm is draped around my shoulder and I'm supporting her with every step. For one of the first times today, I do not know what to do. There is no plan. Logically, I should find a place to sit down, let Carrie recover, and then contact the president. But she's in no shape to hold a conversation right now, and her dad might mistake her for a drunk Delta Delta Delta pledge. No joke.

We reach the end of the alley and I scan the street for a cab. Nipun was kind enough to loan me $20. I really like that kid.

Norfolk's not New-York busy, but it's a pretty big town. Population tops out near 250,000. There's no subway or metro, so I expect on a chilly evening like this the cab drivers will be out looking for cold pedestrians. A police cruiser speeds past us and my heart jumps before I realize they're probably not after us. No civilians will be alerted to what's going on if the director has his way. This will be an inside job. That nondescript black van across the street is more likely to drive onto the sidewalk, yank us in, and drive away than a cop car is. Still scanning for a cab, I stop on the corner of 22nd Street and Broad Street and find myself harkening back to Carrie's mocking question. *Now what?* Where exactly would I tell the cab driver to take us?

When I was a tween, I remember getting into fights with my dad on a regular basis. We were like oil and water. Fire and pine. Bad stuff happened when we butted heads. Those fights generally involved him correcting me and me defending my actions. I'd give it a 50/50 split—he was right half the time and I the other half. Fine, maybe 60/40 his way. As I got older, we'd still have fights, but less frequently. My mother would often ask me afterwards in private, "Ben, what is your point?"

I'd fire back, "What's Dad's point?"

She always encouraged me to "Look deeper, Benjamin. There is always a point." And I would usually find that my point was just to defy my dad, tick him off, or prove I was right just for the sake of it. And I'd look past the fight and see my own pride, my own insecurity. If I could see those flaws, I would repent, seek forgiveness, and move on.

But this is different from all the other fights I've had with my dad. The stakes are greater, and I'm right. The good guys need to win today. I use the word "good" loosely, considering my actions over the past several years.

So as we cross the intersection of 22nd Street and Broad, I listen to my mom and look deeper. I don't have to go that deep. I'm not trying to anger my dad today. I've got no pride left; at least none worth fighting for. And I'm as repentant as a man can be at this point. Today, I've almost destroyed everything I hold dear— my reputation, my job if I make it through this day, hopefully not my relationship with Amy and my kids. The answer has been staring me in the face for the last ten minutes, but my subconscious mind had no interest in this part of the plan because it involves more pain.

I have one more thing to destroy.

I'm a healer—I fix things. That's how this all started anyway, isn't it? I wanted to heal those with diseases that caused memory loss. But that's where this all began, so that's where it should end. I need to go back to the beginning.

A cab finally pulls up to the curb just as my raised arm is beginning to tire. I open the back door and gingerly roll Carrie into the seat. The back seat is warm and smells of coffee and cigarettes. I settle in beside her and put her belt on before securing my own.

"Where to?" the hoarse-voiced cabbie asks, starting the meter.

"Novak Labs," I reply.

I have a master chip to destroy.

Chapter 50
1800

Novak Labs is only a six-minute cab ride away, in the heart of the Eastern Virginia Medical School campus. I feel bad about giving the cab driver a small tip, but the remaining $10 may come in handy later. Carrie is a step closer to coherence but still a babbling mess. My seldom-used office is on the eighteenth floor of the twenty-two-story building. How am I going to get into this building that contains top-secret information and has an armed guard in the lobby and security cameras in every corner?

I'm going to walk right in.

This is becoming somewhat of a recurring theme today.

I tap the glass double doors (which lock after five P.M.) and a guard approaches warily, fingering his holster. When he recognizes me, he returns to his desk and pushes a clandestine button underneath it.

I step confidently through the automatic doors, trying to hide my limp and disguise the impairment of the young lady I'm pulling by the hand. "Ron, long time no see! How's the wife?"

Ron chuckles and shakes his head. "Just fine, Dr. B. It's that teenage daughter I'm worried about!"

I wink at him. "Vanessa's a good girl, you don't have anything to worry about. Plus, you had a shotgun last time I checked."

"Got that right!" he exclaims, cocking an imaginary shotgun before slow clapping and letting out a hearty laugh. "Say, late night for you? You got a . . . student or a special friend with you tonight?" I realize at that moment how awkward I must look pulling an attractive young woman by the hand. She probably doesn't look much older than Vanessa.

I say the first thing that pops into my mind. "My goddaughter, Carrie? Yes, she's never seen the lab so I promised her a private tour." Carrie tries to join the conversation but I cut her off. "Though I fear she's not feeling very well."

"Sorry to hear that. Y'all have fun up there—and young lady, whatever you do, don't push the big red button. Ha, ha!" Ron uses this joke whenever he encounters someone who is new to the building. The truth is, he has no freaking clue what goes on on the eighteenth floor. If he did, he'd ask for a bigger weapon and a raise.

In the elevator, I push the button for the eighteenth floor. Nothing happens until I lean forward and allow the biometric scanner to read my eyes. I type in a code using the elevator buttons. Type it in wrong once and half the agency will arrive within seven minutes. Which reminds me that we probably don't have much time.

On the eighteenth floor, we step into a hallway lined with several doors. The one on the far left leads to the lab, the others to various offices. Mine is the first on the right. I place my forehead against the scanner and my right index finger on a reader.

"Fort Nix?" Carrie asks.

"I think you mean 'Knox'." I suppress a chuckle and walk into my cramped and cluttered office. I always wondered why people put their diplomas on the walls in their offices, as if they've forgotten the schools they attended or can't be bothered to tell people who ask. My walls are covered with art made by my kids, so even when I come to this lab, which is not that often anymore, I feel like I'm at home.

Carrie sits down in my cushioned swivel chair, leans her head back, and groans. I'm sure she has a killer headache but I hope she'll be ready to run in a few minutes. I step behind her and scan the top row of my bookshelf. *Aha, there it is.* I pull down Madeleine L'Engle's *A Wrinkle in Time* and grab the flash drive taped to the back cover. Taking four steps to my right, I scan the bottom shelf and locate Orson Scott Card's *Ender's Game*. I open the front cover and read the message my dad inscribed twenty-two years ago: *To Benjamin—You're never too young to save the world.* I flip to the back cover and pocket the flash drive taped there.

I drop to one knee and open the file cabinet attached to my desk. Some of these files go back to 1999. I see some handwritten notes on Starbucks napkins and remember the day I had a *eureka!* moment in Harvard Square while sharing a Frappuccino with Amy, and the only thing I had to write on was this napkin. I don't have pockets large enough for all these files, CDs, napkins, and books. These memories. But these are the very memories I need to destroy. If there's any information that could lead to the re-creation of the MemSave chip, it must be destroyed. I can't take the chance that the director won't just find someone else to figure this out, but I'm going to make sure he has a hell of a time recreating my work.

I feel sick to my stomach, like this anxiety and grief could LITERALLY burn a hole through my gut. I begin to sweat profusely and clutch my stomach. Then I have an idea.

I'm going to burn it. I'm going to burn it all.

Chapter 51

1810

How do you create a fire in a place that is designed specifically not to burn? There's a sprinkler head in every corner. There are fire extinguishers in every room and along every wall. The floors are fire-retardant. Oh, and then there's the zero-oxygen system that scans a room for signs of life, locks it down, and sucks out the oxygen, extinguishing a fire's lifeblood.

I designed it that way. I couldn't have my life's work go up in flames because of a faulty spark in a lamp, a Bunsen burner gone haywire, or a temp janitor with a smoking habit and a wicked tremor. So the idea that I'm going to burn this stuff is a bit ludicrous. And to be honest, I don't want to destroy this work, these memories. As I thumb through the papers, my vision begins to blur as I'm overcome with emotion. This is the culmination of years, more than a few decades, of research. Blood, sweat, and tears were literally shed for this project to come to life. And not just my own. Chang's. The other post-docs who rotated through the lab over the years. The blood, though . . . that's on my hands. It sullies the good I was trying to do by living out my calling, using my God-given gifts.

What I really want right now is the stuff of movies. For my future self to run into my office wearing a leather jacket from the 2060s and carrying a laser cannon the size of a small Christmas tree. He'll be grey-haired and handsome, of course, in fine physical condition, his face heavily scarred from years of combat. He'll grab me by the shoulders and look me in the eye. "Don't destroy this work. It will change the world. Without the MemSave chip, the world falls into nuclear holocaust and zombie apocalypse!" I'll notice that one of his eyes is fully robotic and wonder what accident caused that and if he's able to see in color or just in black and white. I'll nod my head and tape the flash drives back into their book-cover hiding places. My future self will pause before he walks out of my office and monotonously say, "I'll *not* be back. Hopefully," giving me a slow, dramatic robot eye wink. He'll have seen the same movies I have, so we'll laugh at our joke . . .

And then I'm back to reality, back to my office door after a scavenger hunt though the main laboratory. On my desk are strewn all the papers from my file cabinets. It's a high pile and the flash drives are balanced delicately on top. I nudge the door open with my foot because I'm carrying a high-density polyethylene tub full of papers and other supplies. Carrie is sitting by the door hugging her legs.

"You got a pair of matches, genius?" I'm pleased she's taken to recognizing my intellect but could do without the smart-ass tone.

"Nope, no matches. Here, put this on."

Chapter 52

1815

Sulfuric acid is an odorless, colorless, and incredibly powerful corrosive acid. I remember a silly song a friend of mine used to sing in our chemistry high school class after our teacher warned us repeatedly about the dangers of the acid. "H_2SO_4, I'm thirsty so gimme some more." The teacher did not find this ditty as amusing as we did, but boy, was it fun as high school boys to play with acid. It's amazing to me that every one of us *didn't* become chemists, because Mr. Davis was so engaging, and dissolving anything we could get our grubby hands on was a lot of fun. During my stomach burning moment a few minutes ago, a lightbulb went off in my brain.

How do you burn something in a fireproof lab without starting a fire?

Chemically.

So sulfuric acid was my logical savior, because I don't think I have quite the quantity or concentration of stomach acid to get rid of all this material on my desk.

The HDPE is now stuffed full of papers and topped with flash drives. The Honeywell 8000 full-face respirator I tossed Carrie a few minutes ago now obscures her face save her eyes. They are wide and incredulous. The two of us look ready to either blow something up or make crystal meth. Either way, Walter White would be proud.

"You making me a cappuccino before you do whatever you're about to do?" Carrie rasps through her mask, referring to the handfuls of sugar packets I snagged from the break room. I don't respond as I rip the packets open and sprinkle sugar on top of my pile. She comes over to help. We're done within seconds.

I turn to my desk and hold up a large bottle of concentrated sulfuric acid. I gesture for Carrie to move towards the door. I don't want her to see the tears in my eyes. Here I am, doing what I do best, what I've been doing for the last few years.

Erasing memories.

But this time, I'm going old school; Mr. Davis would be proud.

I'm waiting for my ram-in-the-thicket moment, for God to save me from sacrificing this thing that has been so meaningful, so precious to me. Father Abraham had his only son Isaac, and I have my chip, the only idea I've ever had that was worth a damn. I look in my periphery and see . . . nothing. My ram doesn't appear. My dad's head on a platter doesn't materialize out of thin air. So as I begin to tilt my hand, I'm confident God will stop me from pouring this sulfuric acid onto this sugared pile of flash drives and documentation. My dad will come crashing through these walls with a dozen agents. They'll tackle me and the acid will spill all over the floor, harming nothing but a patch of fire-retardant carpet.

Or . . . no one will stop me. I will pour this acid, and an incredibly powerful exothermic reaction will take place, some of the acid dissolving the contents of the HDPE bin, some of it reacting with the sugar in a dehydration process that removes the water from the sugar and produces a great deal of heat and steam. For centuries, religious writers and artists depicted hell as a lake of fire and sulfur. In some way, this bucket of sulfuric acid represents hell—a place far from the presence of God and good.

I watch it all burn and transform into a disturbing black mess, the radiating heat warming my face despite the mask.

It's time to go. I go to my bookshelf and pick up a book. I look at the inscription one last time, then turn and toss it into hell.

You're never too old to save the world. Or yourself.

Chapter 53

1820

I am a little surprised by the ease with which we walk out of Novak Labs. No tactical team, no sirens. Just a goodnight to Ron and the push of a button to let us out the sliding doors. Not that I'm complaining. Carrie and I still have a bit of work to do. I did not want to call the president or the director until we'd destroyed the physical components that could lead to future chip manufacture. *Check.*

But there is always a "What if?"

What if, when I deactivated our chips in the mainframe, they weren't truly disabled? What if my dad is able to find someone skilled enough to crack the code—and I'm sure that person is out there—and they can reactivate our chips? Or activate the kill switch? How will I be able to sleep at night knowing that at any point I might not wake up? Or I might drop dead in front of my wife and kids?

That's not living. Even though I'm only working on a hunch, it's a hunch that could save my life. I share my thoughts with Carrie as we cross the street. "We need to make sure our chips are truly deactivated. I don't think we can take a chance that someone won't figure out how to activate them again."

Carrie punches me in the arm and I stop in the middle of the crosswalk.

"You are NOT cutting off my ear," she yells, poking me in the chest.

I walked into that one. What else was she supposed to think?

"Is that why we're walking towards Sentara General Hospital? So someone can sew our ears back on after they take the chip out?" She is correct about our destination. This biomedical complex includes Novak Labs, Children's Hospital of the King's Daughters, and Sentara General Hospital. I try to reassure her as I pull her by the arm across the street towards the bright neon lights of the hospital entrance.

"No one else is going to lose an ear today, I promise." Saying that makes me laugh a bit. One of my favorite Bible stories growing up was of Jesus in the garden of Gethsemane. In one version of the story, when Jesus is confronted by the Roman soldiers and Judas the betrayer looks on, a disciple pulls a knife and cuts off the ear of one of the soldiers. For whatever reason, my six-year-old brain pictured this lopped-off ear falling to the ground, doing a little jig, and then letting Jesus pick it up and place it back on the injured soldier's head. The lesson I took from the story was of Jesus' compassion even for the soldiers coming to lead him to his death. That in the midst of betrayal, he was still a compassionate healer.

I'm no Jesus. I've got a hell of a lot of Judas in me. I've betrayed just about everyone I know and love over the past few years—and especially today. My thoughts go to Amy, Angela, Carrie, Kwasi, the people standing outside in the cold at the naval hospital. My dad would argue I've betrayed my country today.

But I'm still trying to fix this. I'm trying to heal things. And if I'm going to be crucified for my actions today, I want to die with a clear conscience. Part of that is making sure Carrie, Angela, and those that I love who have microchips aren't victimized again. It's why I told Carrie to make sure the doctors order an MRI. Demand it, because that powerful magnet may be the only thing strong enough to make the MemSave chip permanently malfunction.

Chapter 54

1831

I haven't told Carrie that there's a possibility the MRI scanner could rip the microchip right out of her ear.

Details.

I could probably spend hours telling her what a magnetic resonance imaging machine is capable of. How it's able to scan the human body and provide an unmatched level of detail. How the field strength of the magnet can reach upwards of three Tesla. How the powerful radio transmitter that produces the electromagnetic field might be—and I emphasize the word *might*—strong enough to completely disrupt the MemSave chip.

Instead, I just tell her we have to get into a giant tube-shaped magnet machine for ten to twenty minutes to short-circuit the memory-wiping microchips in our ears.

I walk us confidently through the emergency room doors and past the triage desk. Even though I don't look very doctor-like right now in a hoodie and cargo pants, I'm prepared to say, "I'm Dr. Brew, and I have an emergency," if anyone tries to stop me. I have found over the years that a little confidence in a hospital setting goes a long way. Showing up to a precipitous baby delivery with a calm face, stethoscope in hand, tends to put a room full of anxious people at ease. Carrie is used to people parting the sea for her, so she's not that impressed, but she does ask, "So we're just going to walk right into the MRI? Are there like twenty of them in the basement?" as we step into a staff-only elevator.

We are headed to the basement. I wait for the doors to close before I answer. "Most hospitals have two scanners, maybe three. This is a Level 1 trauma center so I suspect there are at least three. They always try to leave one or two open for emergencies, and the third one is used for scheduled scans. We might have to bump someone who's coming in for a non-urgent scan. Luckily I'm good friends with one of the radiologists. Let's hope he's on call."

I am relieved to see Dr. Erik Moore working at his station when we enter the MRI suite.

"Brew, I texted you about watching the Vikings-Pats game last night but never heard from you," he says, staring at his screen. "You didn't miss much. Your Vikings still suck."

He and I do not need pleasantries. We usually just get right to the point. That's how it is when you've known somebody for fifteen years and spent time in training together. We did our internship together in pediatrics, but Erik didn't like the politics of the department or having to deal with irresponsible parents, so he jumped ship to radiology after intern year.

"Sorry I missed your call, dude. It's been a . . . busy twenty-four hours. I wish I had time for small talk but we're on a tight schedule." I place my hand on Carrie's shoulder. "Erik, meet Carrie Banning." Erik raises an eyebrow. "Yeah, *the* Carrie Banning. She and I need to get brain MRIs pronto. I can't explain why—but it's a matter of national security. Can you get us into two scanners now?" I'm talking a mile a minute, but we're running out of time. The director could have already figured out how to pull the plug, and maybe he's just waiting to figure out how much we've shared. We've got to get this done before we make contact with them. Even if it's just a hunch that this magnet can actually deactivate the chips.

"Brew, I love you, but you're ridiculously optimistic if you think I have two MRIs free on a Friday evening. The best I can get you is one, in about four minutes, when this nineteen-year-old suspected ACL tear is done. I can run a thirty-minute brain scan on both of you. In total you should be out of here in a little over an hour," he says, tapping his wristwatch.

That's way too long.

I wring my hands. "We only have about twenty minutes . . . but that'll have to do. Let's do this."

The moment the patient in Scanner #3 is done, I make a beeline for the imaging room, pulling Carrie behind me. "Oh, I didn't know they were that . . . small," she pines.

"This is a bad time to be claustrophobic, Carrie. We've got to get in. *Now.*" And for a moment I'm telling Gabriella that she has to sit in the dentist's chair to get her cavities filled. And she's looking at me with those big brown eyes. And I steel myself against the emotions welling up in me, because there's a job that must be done. I point to the chair and tell Gabri to *Get in, right n—*

Erik's voice comes in over the intercom and I snap my head to see him sitting at the computer on the other side of the thick window, busily making keystrokes. "For your safety, I have to make sure you have removed all metal from your person, since you are getting inside a powerful magnet. No metal penile implants, right, Brew?"

I would ordinarily find that amusing but today I'm not in the mood. I yell back, "We're both good," as I lie down on the gurney. The technician is about to roll me in when I tell him to stop. "C'mon, Carrie, let's go."

She looks at me quizzically. "You mean . . . right now? With you?" And she finally understands why I have been using the word "we" for the last ten minutes. Because "we" need to get this done right now. There's no time for two separate MRIs. I gesture her over again. She walks over slowly and climbs onto the gurney, kneeling. The tech is mortified; we have obviously strayed waaaay off protocol.

"You serious, Brew? Y'all could just get a room." Erik's voice echoes in the imaging suite. "And the images are going to be pretty crappy. Not the ones I'm taking on my cell phone right now to show Amy, but the ones of your brain." He adds a *z* sound to *brain* as he finishes his thought.

"I don't need pictures, Erik. Just the magnet. Turn the darn thing on!" I reach my hand out towards Carrie. She takes it . . . and then lies down on top of me, her head on my shoulder. I give the tech the thumbs-up to wheel us in.

Suffice it to say, it is a tight fit. I feel Carrie's warm breath on my cheek. Not the first time today I've been in an intimate position with the opposite sex. If I make it through this day, I will brag to Amy about my incredible self-control. If I make it. But the truth is, there's nothing even remotely romantic about this moment. I've been knocked out cold, dodged bullets, vomited on myself, and survived a major car accident that ended at the bottom of a river. Oh, and my wife cut off my ear. Just today. It's going to take a lot more than a moment like this to get a rise out of me. I could use a hot shower, a plate of crispy bacon and over easy eggs, and a nice warm bed to pass out on. My hormones, along with the rest of my body, may need a couple of days to recuperate.

I can't speak for Carrie, but since I'm old enough to be her dad and have always treated her like one of my own daughters, I hope what she feels is . . . cared for. I hear her breathing fast and tell her to calm down, that she's safe, that everything's going to be all right. I tell her to ignore the instructions that we remain perfectly still, since our only goal is to disrupt the microchips in our ears. I tell her that my trick to surviving an MRI (I've had several since injuring my lower back playing basketball in high school) is to sing my favorite album. Mine back then was Weezer's *The Blue Album*. Clocking in at forty-one minutes and seventeen seconds, singing that entire album in my head could get me just about through an entire MRI session from start to finish. I'd repeat track seven, *Say It Ain't So*, just for fun because it was my favorite song. I interpreted the lyrics to be about a son struggling with his dad's drinking habit and facing his own inner demons. I'm struggling with my own demons today, having inherited my dad's habit of wanting to control everything. My mom, my brother, my behavior . . . the country. Becoming director of the agency was the closest he could get to controlling the country without becoming president. I always choked up when I sang the line, "This way . . . is a waterslide away from me that takes you further every day." Because that's how it felt every time he tried to exert control. Now it's easier to call him Director Brew than Dad. But that's the wrong song for this moment.

Carrie is shivering. Don't know if she's cold or scared or what. So I begin to sing softly to her, and I feel her body relaxing. I'm loosening up, too. She giggles as I recreate the opening dialogue of *The Sweater Song*, and I'm giggling as she joins me in the chorus, having foolishly thought her way too young to know who or what Weezer is. As we sing "Watch me unravel, I'll soon be naked, lying on the floor, I come undone" at the top of our voices, Erik joins in over the intercom, the loud clanking of the MRI magnet providing percussion. It's a motley moment, for sure; one I'll remember for a while, I hope.

We finish the song and I decide it's been enough. The tech rolls us out of the machine and Carrie peels herself off of me. "I think I was starting to get a little too comfortable in there," she remarks as she tucks her shirt back into her pants.

"I don't know what you're talking about. I was asleep the whole time. What happened?" We both erupt with laughter, and I realize it's the first time today I have felt genuinely happy. I nonchalantly feel my right ear and it seems intact. If the chip had been sucked out of my ear I am sure I would have felt it, so I just have to hope twenty minutes was enough.

Erik and I bro-hug outside in the control room and I promise to catch up with him later. He makes me promise or he'll send out the compromising pictures of me. Such a tease. He lets me tinker on his computer for a minute before we part ways. I find what I need and release a sigh of relief.

Carrie follows me back to the patient elevator and we take it to the eleventh floor. I step out and scan the hall. We walk right past the nurses' station to Room 1114. Carrie asks, "Who are we here to see? Another one of your buddies?"

I give the door two quick raps and push it open, making way for Carrie to walk in first.

She gasps and starts to sob. Happy sobs, I think, with just enough space in between to briefly speak.

"Hi, Angie."

Chapter 55

1859

This is a typical hospital room. The lighting is dim but there isn't much to see. Beige walls, one window, a mini TV attached to a mechanical arm that glides over the bed. The door to the bathroom is slightly ajar. There's a tray table on wheels topped with an untouched copy of today's *Virginian Pilot*. I could be the headline tomorrow, unfortunately. The room smells antiseptic, a nauseating mix of Betadine and bleach. A couple of oversized faux leather chairs that probably convert to sleepers flank Angela's bed.

Angela opens her eyes at the sound of Carrie's voice. "I told the front desk I wasn't expecting any visitors. The security in this joint sucks." Angela's weary face feigns disappointment before breaking into a wide smile. Carrie steps up to her battered friend and begins gently stroking her hair like a mother would a sleeping child. She's never seen Angela like this. I haven't either. If I didn't know any better, I'd have assumed she was on the wrong end of a boxing bout or a mugging. Angela and Carrie spend a few minutes swapping stories while I scout out the room and locate the hallway exits in case we need to escape. We shouldn't if this phone call goes well.

I break up the girls' conversation and ask them if they are ready to talk to the most powerful man in America—or in Carrie's words, her "a-hole father." I think she's ready. Angela looks to be fading out again, and I squint to read the labels on her IV bags. Whoa, I'm surprised she even woke up to talk at all. Carrie grabs the handset on Angela's tray table and begins to dial her dad's secure line. I hear President Banning answer after the first ring. There is some static in the line as Carrie puts the phone on speaker.

"Carrie, I've been worried sick about you. Are you ok? Are you hurt?"

"In more ways than you think, Dad."

What a sad bunch we are. Here I am sitting beside the First Daughter on speakerphone with the president of the United States, my own dad no doubt patched in and listening. Just two messed-up dads having a conversation with their messed-up children. Carrie's conversation with her dad? Could have been me twenty years ago. Now my dad wouldn't dare ask if I was ok or hurt. We're waaaay past that. I hope POTUS treads carefully here—the words he says to his daughter have the potential to save their relationship . . . or completely destroy it.

"I am sorry about what happened to the consul general," he says flatly. And then his tone intensifies. "That . . . that wasn't part of the plan. In the heat of the moment, I panicked. I listened to my advisor and made . . . the wrong call." He swears under his breath, and overall he sounds apologetic, though I wish I could see his face. But is he really going to stop listening to his "advisor," aka my dad?

"Can we go back to the day you decided it was ok to put a chip in my ear that screws up my memory? How could you?" Carrie is almost in hysterics, now standing over the phone. "Why couldn't you just talk to me like an adult, hear me out, and then trust me to make the right choice?"

"Because there was so much at stake, Carrie. I didn't want you to have to make any choice," he states, his voice rising. "I'm the president of the United States. The chip program was MY decision to make, not yours. I'm responsible for the citizens of this country, for national security. I didn't want that weight on you, Carrie. I figured if you just forgot that you ever heard about the chip program, that you'd just let it go."

"So you took away my ability to choose?" she shouts back. "And you lied to Dr. Brew and told him I was still using drugs—which I'm not. So you made me feel like I was crazy. I was never sure when I had taken my prescribed meds. So when I had my five-minute tonic-clonic seizure today? That was your fault." She slams her palm on the tray table, causing Angela's eyes to briefly flutter open.

Carrie doesn't notice, and I'm glad she isn't mincing words. I nod at her reassuringly and she continues.

"You're going to end this program, Dad. Because it's wrong. And I'm not the president, but I am your daughter. And you claim to love me. And you've raised me to believe that my opinion and feelings matter, that integrity matters. It's what you told me when you were running for president—that you wanted me to be proud of you. Right now, I think you know how I feel. I don't deserve this. Those troops don't deserve this. My friend didn't deserve to see her dad die in front of her," her voice escalating to a fever pitch. "You killed him! And that's wrong!"

She's standing over the phone holding herself and sobbing, and I hope the walls in this private room are thick enough or that the patients in the adjoining rooms look a lot worse than Angela. Maybe they'll just think we have the TV turned up loud and we're watching an episode of *Scandal*.

As the president responds, I hear something in his voice. He's broken.

"I want to fix this, Carrie. I'm so . . . so sorry. But . . . but I do need to know who else you've spoken to. For security reasons. If I decommission this program, I need to understand how widespread the information is so I c—"

"So you can kill the people who I've spoken to? I think you've got that covered," she responds venomously. She slowly lowers herself back into the chair.

"No, so I can *contain* the information. This could cause war, Carrie. A lot of people could die. And I'm not trying to belittle you, but I'm not sure you fully grasp the scope of how bad an information leak would be in this situation. Your trip to the *Virginian Pilot* really concerned me. I'm glad we got there before you were able to write too much down."

"You read my written statement? You broke the law to r—"

"I utilized executive privilege, Carrie. So yes, I read your very brief statement and there wasn't much to it. It's thankfully harmless."

My stomach churns as I feel my plan falling to pieces. I hadn't even stopped to ask Carrie how far she got in her statement. She was too out of it forty-five minutes ago for me to pose any questions that I wanted coherent answers to. I decide it's time to show my hand.

"I take it you didn't see my statement then, Mr. President? The one that Bill Simons has been instructed to immediately release to the press if he doesn't hear my voice every thirty minutes?"

Silence.

I let my words sink in. "I need to be able to confirm that the chip program is done. I need full access to the mainframe. I don't care if the director is there, but he can't interfere. He perverted my work, and I let him. Did he tell you about the side effects, Mr. President? The troops that are blind and deaf because of this chip? Curing PTSD? Ha! We've traumatized these troops, and they deserve better." I'm surprised the director hasn't chimed in. Maybe he's in the president's doghouse because of how bungled today's operation has been, beginning with erasing twenty-two years of my memories. "I need complete access to the mainframe so I can shut this down."

"You'll have it, Brew. You have my word," he replies. "But can I see you, Carrie? I just want to see you. Give you a hug. Let you see how sorry I really am."

Carrie looks at me, confused. "Sure, Dad, I was planning on coming up to DC during my winter break next week anyway. I can come sooner, I guess."

"Don't worry about that. I've come to you. Air Force One is landing right now."

I'm figuring out how Carrie and I will get to the Langley Air Force Base helipad and then to the agency when the president speaks again.

"I'll see you in five minutes."

What? I jog over to the door and poke my head out. The hallways are quiet. Too quiet.

"How?" Carrie blurts out.

"We've landed on the hospital helipad. After the security sweep I'll be right in."

POTUS is full of surprises today.

Chapter 56

1925

My heart beats rapidly because I'm about to encounter the Secret Service. I'm probably not their favorite person right now. I've deceived some of their agents today and two of their colleagues are at the bottom of the James River, which I feel terrible about. And depending on the spin the director and the president have put on it, they probably have no idea what's going on, why I've done what I've done.

Doctors save lives. It's what I've been trying to do all day, but I haven't done a very good job of it, except for saving my own, and Angela's, and Carrie's.

So is this just another power play by POTUS? Will he call my bluff about the press release? Bill Simons has nothing from me. No doubt he's already sent a team to the newspaper's office to verify my claim. If I die in the next few minutes, the story of the MemSave chip dies with me. Chang? I hope he's somewhere far, far from here, because there's no way he emerges unscathed. The director will find a way to quiet him. And Angela. And Carrie. And Amy? No, he'll leave her alone. He'll assume I didn't tell her anything to keep her safe, or that she'd be too scared to admit she knew anything.

And if my MRI theory didn't work, my father will find a way to use the chip. He'll find a definitive way to shut me up. If he really believes there's any chance I'll go to the press, he won't take any chances. I just hope he'll have the courtesy to make it quick. There's no need for some long, drawn-out interrogation. Maybe the agents will take me into an empty hospital room and do it quietly.

How poetic. For a doctor to die in a hospital. I suppose many of us do.

How . . . *terrifying*. The thought never really crossed my mind until now. Sure, I've been a patient before for minor procedures, most recently my vasectomy. Three children has stretched me. Four would dismember me completely, one to rip each limb. But to die here? In a building where I've witnessed so much life and death? As a pediatric resident, I participated in hundreds upon hundreds of delivery-room and operating-room births. They weren't all happy beginnings. I participated in my fair share of failed resuscitations, cared for babies with congenital anomalies not compatible with life or with perinatal insults too devastating to overcome.

There's no one here to resuscitate me. No one will call a Code Blue. I'm sure the final autopsy will state that I expired from natural causes—or maybe they'll dramatically call me an enemy of the state, blame me for the consul general's death. I'm sure there's video evidence that can be corrupted. Amy and the girls will be pariahs. They'll have to change their last names, relocate, create a new life for themselves.

I sit at Angela's bedside holding her hand as she swoons in a drug-induced stupor. Carrie sits wordlessly beside me waiting for the door to open and her dad to walk in. Resignation sets in. I think this could be the end.

I've gotten myself out of quite a few jams today, but there's no escaping now. The moment Air Force One landed on the helipad, agents were already making this floor one of the safest places in the world, temporarily. Anywhere the president travels is generally one of the safest places in the world—the agency makes it that way. It's their job.

I stand up and drop to my knees, locking my hands behind my head. There's no doubt in my mind that agents are outside the door right now. They've already done thermal and infrared scans of the room. They'll know there are three warm bodies in here but won't know if I am armed. My position of surrender will help answer that question. From my side of Angela's bed, I can see Carrie's arms from the elbows up trembling in the air as she follows my lead.

The door opens and three agents enter, guns drawn. In seconds they scan the room and frisk me and Carrie. One of them taps his earpiece and gives the all-clear.

And in walks the president of the United States.

Chapter 57

1930

You don't become president of the United States without knowing how to command a room. It does help having armed men point guns at your audience, but President Banning is a fit, well-groomed fifty-year-old man. Young by presidential standards. Post-election polling revealed that his "attractiveness factor" played a key role in his victory two Novembers ago. His policies weren't so bad, either.

POTUS, in a two piece black suit and crimson silk tie, marches straight to Carrie and envelops her in his arms. I can hear her sobbing into his chest, and soon his sobs join hers. It's a tender moment, and my heart aches to hold Amy and Ana and Gabri and Kobi. I may never hold them again.

Then I remember Amy's words to me the last time we were together at the house. *Do what you have to do to keep me and the girls safe*. Hasn't that been the goal of every waking moment of my life since I said "I do"? Well, every waking moment except this morning, since I had no idea what the heck was going on when I woke up.

So I'll heed Amy's words in this moment. I'll do what it takes to keep her and the girls safe. I'll play the president's game. For the moment, I'm still alive, so I must be playing the game correctly . . . I just need to figure out the rules.

Carrie and her dad are now looking into each other's eyes, speaking in hushed whispers. I imagine they are rehashing a lot of what has happened today. There's genuine sorrow in the president's face, which is another good sign. Voters also said they thought Senator Banning was "genuine," and they were right about that. He doesn't have a very good poker face, but that's because he usually plays with an open hand. Unless the director is in the picture. And as far as I can tell, my dad's not here.

President Banning turns to me and his words catch me off guard.

"Thank you, Benjamin. For keeping Carrie safe. For helping me undo some of the damage I've done."

It feels weird to hear the leader of the free world taking ownership of his mistakes. Perhaps it's easier because there are no congressmen or cameras around. He's graciously left out the fact that it was my idea to insert the chip into Carrie, probably because he feels guilty for manipulating me after the chip did what I intended it to do: curb her enthusiasm for drugs. His lies about her continued drug abuse covered his (and the director's) true intent. I've always believed that with my dad present, anyone can be two-faced. Honest Abe would have never earned his nickname with my dad at his side.

The president rubs his daughter's shoulders and kisses her forehead. "Wait for me outside," he tells her, longingly watching her walk towards the door, acutely aware of how close he was to losing her today, both emotionally and corporeally. "Wait outside," he orders the agents standing watch.

I'm not sure I've ever been alone in a room with POTUS. Initially, the silence is uncomfortable, but the longer we sit here, the longer I'm alive. *I'm still in the game*.

"We screwed up, your dad and I. You'll have to talk to him yourself, but he knows how I feel. This all went way too far. I didn't know about the side effects. And to be honest, I didn't want to know, because Benjamin, I thought we had a real shot at true world peace." We sit across from each other on opposite sides of Angela's bed.

"Can you imagine, Benjamin? Controlling negotiations by eliminating key parts of the other side's memory? If things went south during a conversation, you hit the reset button and start again the next day using a different tactic. I truly believed that with some refinement, we'd have been able to use the chip as a tool for peace. Not the weapon that it is today. I . . . I truly had no idea about the kill switch. You think I'd have placed one in Carrie if I knew there was a chance it could kill her?" He's gripping the sheets tightly, his face contorted in anguish. I stay neutral as I process this information.

"Mr. President, I can't speak for my father, but like many of the things the agency does, not telling you about the kill switch allowed you plausible deniability. If things went to pot, which arguably they have, you wouldn't know. Yeah, it would be under your watch, but you wouldn't be subject to prosecution from the fallout. We were just trying to pro—"

"Protect me." He chuckles and shakes his head. "We should all be sainted . . . or knighted. It seems like we're all just trying to protect someone. We're knights of the republic, protecting the American people. My daughter. Each other. How does protecting someone get so screwed up?"

"Because generally," I counter, "when we say we're protecting someone else, we're usually just protecting ourselves. Or at the very least, we're doing it selfishly— to make ourselves feel better, give ourselves some moral high ground."

"Well, we've dug ourselves quite a moral pit, wouldn't you say?" I nod. He couldn't be more right.

In that moment, I realize erasing memories is as dangerous as the movies make time travel seem. Rule #1 of time travel? Any change you make has a ripple effect for the future. Change a person's memories? They won't have that memory to inform their future behavior. Boy, had my dad exploited that, sending troops into multiple high-risk engagements because they didn't remember they'd just been in one. Hell, I'd done it to myself. Erased my own memories of toying with soldiers' brains, so I could continue . . . toying with soldiers' brains. Relatively guilt free, so I thought. But I don't think you can erase guilt. Those seeds are planted way deeper than memories. The uneasiness I felt all day, before I got my memories back? That was guilt gnawing at my innards.

This all began because I was trying to cure PTSD. I'm a doctor first, soldier second. But in trying to cure PTSD, I gave my dad the power to do far worse.

I complete my inner monologue and realize that the president has stopped speaking. So I fill the uncomfortable silence.

"Let's dig ourselves out of this pit. I'll handle my father; he and I have a lot to discuss."

"Yes, you do. I'm sure you're angry with him. But please know that he loves you. He's never more proud than when he talks about all you've achieved. You're his hero, like Carrie's mine. When you have children—and you know this as a father and pediatrician—you want your children to be better than you. To not make the mistakes you did. To bring out the best in you. You and Carrie have done that today."

I'm surprised to hear this. A warmth begins to fill my icy chest. Some would call this feeling hope. "Thank you for sharing that with me, Mr. President. I acknowledge and regret my role in all this. I hope that I can make things right."

Banning stands and places a hand on my shoulder and our eyes meet. "You can, and you will. We have a lot of damage control to do, so let's get going. The director is waiting for us back at the agency." He flicks his head in Langley's direction. "Let's get you to that mainframe."

Chapter 58

1954

I manage to bandage up a few of my wounds before leaving Angela's hospital room, and I kiss her on the forehead before being escorted out. The hallways and windowed doors are lined with the stunned faces of nurses and patients hoping to get a look at the president of the United States. It's a moment I'm sure they'll remember for the rest of their lives.

Remember. Memories.

Banning flashes his presidential smile and waves to the wide-eyed spectators. Secret Service doesn't let him shake any hands as they flank him, carefully scanning for threats.

Minutes later, we are climbing into Air Force One. In front of me, Carrie shields her ears from the humming *wumpf wumpf* of the rotor blades. I find my way to the back row and put on the bulky noise-dampening headphones.

The ride to the agency gives me time to process and rest. I've been running all day but I feel like this is almost over. And by *this*, I mean this Godforsaken day of misery. I've already given thanks to God for not letting me end up in the hospital morgue, which was a pleasant surprise. I've spoken with Amy and told her to turn around and come back home. She was relieved to hear my voice and more relieved to know the conflict is over. Almost.

A part of me regrets that she knows about the safe house now, and about my secret-agent life, but I'm actually a little relieved to not have to keep secrets anymore.

I look out the helicopter window and survey the landscape. The buildings, the houses, the roads, the trees—everything appears so small from this bird's-eye view. All the people in those buildings, those houses, on those roads—they have no idea what's gone on today. The general public operates under a shroud of ignorance 99% of the time, and I think people like it that way. A few years back when Ed Snowden shared some of the deeper secrets of how the government intrudes on privacy, people were outraged—for a minute. Then we all went back to using our cell phones and laptops because, to be honest? Government intrusion really didn't interfere with our lives. We could still watch football on Sundays, drink beer and smoke weed in our homes, have romantic relations with whoever we desired, and die in hospitals with our families at our bedsides. Life went on as usual.

What would the public say if they knew about the chip program? Paranoia would set in at first as everyone wondered whether they were chipped or not. It would be a great time to own MRI stock. Then everyone would want to know who controlled the chip, and if that person could be trusted. If the president's dream had come true, we'd have ushered in world peace but wouldn't be able to tell anyone how. Everything we'd accomplished would be unraveled, because when you manipulate someone for a righteous cause, the means do not justify the end. Because if that person truly knows and loathes the means, then regardless of the outcome, you haven't created meaningful change. Research has proven that when you spank a child to stop a negative behavior, you haven't created a meaningful change. You've stopped the negative behavior, but you've also created resentment.

And that's the thing about our memories. They *always* meaningfully change us, for better or for worse. We're capable of making choices based on those memories. History does repeat itself, but it's because memory generally sucks. Memory is unfaithful. Memory is history's fickle lover. If memory was faithfully married to history, we'd never forget. We wouldn't make the same mistakes. Or if we did, it'd be completely by choice, not because we stupidly forgot.

But memory is that girl that leaves you for long periods of time, and when she returns, you're not sure whether to be happy or sad. Sometimes she makes you feel so warm inside, reminds you of everything good about yourself. And other times she shows you the evil you've done, that you wish you could forget but you can't. But in the end, you know one thing to be true: You can't live without her.

And as you get older, you miss her more and more, and when she's present you cherish her. And you draw more on physical things—albums, written stories, oral tales—to bring her back.

The longer this day gets, and the further I get from having part of my ear lopped off, more of my memories return. And they're beautiful. My eyes well up with tears thinking about them. The good ones and the bad ones. They're all beautiful. I think of all the post-traumatic growth I've had from my bad experiences, and I wonder how I could ever have thought that curing PTSD by erasing my memories of trauma was the right answer.

We touch down at the agency and I say a quick prayer as I prepare to face my biggest adversary, the man who has traumatized me today in ways I couldn't imagine.

Joseph Alexander Brew.

Chapter 59

2016

Two agents escort me off the roof and down a secure stairwell that smells of metal and gasoline. Before I got off the helicopter, the president allowed me to place a phone call to the *Virginian Pilot*. Bill Simons played along at the other end of the line, keeping my bluff intact. In fact, the president was the one who reminded me to make the phone call, so I'm confident he took me seriously. He's not staying for the fireworks with my dad, though; he opts to take his daughter out for dinner instead. Maybe Dad and I will grab a bite after all this?

The agents flanking me have no idea why I am laughing out loud right now, and from their faces I can tell I've made them a bit uneasy.

We enter a service elevator at the bottom of the stairwell. As the doors close, I look at each agent out of my periphery. I'm not restrained, and they simply stand at parade rest, their hands locked behind their backs. But I know better than to let down my guard. I'm in the dragon's lair, and I need to be prepared for fire. I watch the level indicator drop until it reaches -1.

The mainframe.

I appreciate this nonviolent escort into the bowels of the agency. I'm tired of fighting today. My dad greets me at the door of the mainframe as I fight off a feeling of déjà vu.

"Are you happy with yourself?" His opening salvo stings. It takes me back to childhood, to times where after I'd made a mistake, Dad would pose a rhetorical question. Rhetorical because the one time I did answer affirmatively, he slapped my face and my lip bled for twenty minutes. I was eight.

It's been thirty-two years ... Hmmm. What the hell?

"Yes, yes I am," I respond, a smug smile spreading across my face.

My dad almost chokes on his own spit, then lunges at me. I fully expect him to slap me, but in a flash the agents are in front of me, blocking his way.

They're protecting me! I almost laugh out loud for the second time in the last minute, but I compose myself and pat them on the shoulders. "It's ok, he can't hurt me." They relax and step aside. I walk past my dad into the mainframe, the footsteps of my bodyguards close behind me.

And there it is. The computer terminal that controls everything. I know what I need to do, but I need to talk to my dad first. I have a lot to say. I'm sure he does, too.

This conversation will not only be top secret, but personal. Very personal. I turn to the agents and thank them for their service. I tell them to wait outside the door and to come back in twenty minutes so I can make a call to the *Virginian Pilot*. They nod and walk out of the room.

So now it's just the two of us.

"The *Virginian Pilot*? A nice bluff. The president bought it . . . did you really think your old man would?" He shakes his head in apparent disbelief. "You're too smart to do something that dumb. Something to put Amy and the kids in danger. The press would have to name their source, and then they'd come for your family. You know how high the stakes are. So let's stop playing games."

"We've never stopped playing games, Dad," I spit back. "The game started before you involuntarily placed a first-generation microchip in my ear twenty-two years ago. It continued when you used it to erase my memories. But it does end now, because I'm putting a stop to your BS. It's time to shut it down."

Chapter 60

2021

We are two caged fighters, our cage this mainframe room. We circle each other menacingly, knowing that only one of us will emerge victorious.

"What about the soldiers?" he asks. He must not know that I've seen the side effects of the chip up close and personal.

"It's all about the soldiers, Dad. We've ruined them, they're damaged goods. Yeah, we had some success on the battlefield. But look at them. They can't see. They can't hear. They are shells of their former selves. Erasing the trauma has traumatized them even more!"

"ISIS. Boko Haram. North Korea." My dad lifts the fingers on his raised hand one at a time. "Successful covert missions not possible without the chip. You can't deny the results. They volunteered. They are government property," he says with an air of finality.

"Joining the military isn't volunteering to be dehumanized. These are men and women with families. With hopes and dreams. They deserve better." I'm trying not to raise my voice, but I'm getting angrier.

"So by your logic, we just turn off their chips? Let all their memories back? Talk about retraumatization. You have a clinic with psychiatrists skilled enough to handle the fallout?" he smirks.

I shake my head. "We're not talking hundreds of troops, Dad. Less than fifty, if my glance at that mainframe earlier is any indication. No, we give them *choice*, which we should have done from the beginning. We bring them in slowly, maybe eight at a time, and explain to them what's been done. And then we give them the option of having the chip turned off. Some of them won't want to relive the trauma, you're right. Others will want to know what they did, why they feel so messed up. I even suspect that giving some of them their memories back will *fix* some of the side effects. But the bottom line? They've got to have a choice." My dad's face is blank as he processes this. He's always been difficult to read, and today is no different.

He scratches his temple and looks down at the floor. "Fine. So that takes care of the soldiers. But they must maintain their secrecy about the missions," he says, lifting his face, his eyes filled with anger. "We can't have them going rogue like some of those Seal Team Six members after the Bin Laden raid. We control the information flow, we con—"

"We can't control everything. We tried to, and look where that's gotten us. I'm sure if anything important leaks out, you and your friends in the media-relations division can spin your way out of it. This isn't a negotiation, Dad. I'm telling you how it's going to be."

He stiffens, and I think reality is setting in for him. He may still be the director after all this, but his power over me, over the president, over this particular program, ends today.

"How it's going to be, eh?" he mimics, rubbing his chin pensively. "Are we bringing in the ayatollah as well? The Russian ambassadors? The Canadian PM?" And I really don't want to believe him that the program has gone that far, but I've already seen what's been done with Consul General Wang. And as far as inventory, I haven't accounted for all the chips. If he's not bluffing, and those MemSave chips are really functioning in some our closest allies and gravest enemies, then I have only one answer.

"No. We're not bringing them in. But I'm not letting you use the chips anymore either."

"THIS IS WAR!" he screams, stomping emphatically and adding some choice expletives. "You think the Iranians or the Russians aren't trying to infiltrate our government right now? Look at what the Chinese are doing now! You think they wouldn't use this same technology, if it was in their hands, to cripple us? How naïve are you? I didn't raise a damn idiot!"

He is right. They would use it to take us down. And as much as I want to say that we're better than them, to lean on that faithful crutch of American exceptionalism, the truth is . . . we're not. We are not better than them. We love our country and our way of life as much as they love theirs. They love their children as much as we love ours. Perhaps their record on human rights isn't stellar, but we're not without reproach either.

"But Dad, it's been over seventy-five years since an atomic bomb was dropped. We could have done it again, but we haven't. Because we decided there were better ways to fight. We didn't just go around nuking our enemies."

"You're making my point for me, Ben," he retorts, his face animated. "The chip is so much less destructive than a nuclear device. It's targeted. It's practically diplomatic. We literally talked our way out of war a few months ago by just a few selective memory wipes of intense negotiations. We could have fixed this China crisis by the weekend. We can stop bloodshed. We never have to use nuclear weapons again. You've done it! Your work as an undergrad and beyond. We would have never been able to achieve this without you!"

His voice is trembling as he steps towards me, gripping me by the shoulders. Curiously, I don't feel like he's about to body-slam me. I see tears in his eyes. Either this is his greatest performance or my dad is genuinely moved. Sadly, I believe it's the former. He isn't crying because he's proud of me. He's crying for the chip program because it's about to die. And his attempts to flatter me, to make me feel proud of something that I created, fall flat.

He can see it in my eyes. His brow furrows, as if he's thinking of asking me to reconsider, but he knows it is too late. America must be better. We have always found another way, and we will again.

A tear falls from his eye and I watch it roll down his cheek into his grey beard. In that split second, I miss the narrowing of his eyes that signals the shift in his attitude, and I'm not ready for the pull of his hands on my shoulders that bring my head down on his rising knee.

In the dragon's lair . . .

Chapter 61

2031

For a sixty seven-year-old man, my dad is in phenomenal shape. He ran the Navy-Marine Corps Marathon two years ago and placed in the top ten in his age division. Right now, I wish he was a fat, out-of-shape old geezer. I turn my head just in time to absorb the brunt of his kneecap with my left cheekbone, which breaks with a stomach-curdling *thump.*

My head bounces back up and I immediately feel his fist in my solar plexus. The breath rushes out of my lungs, and before I have time to inhale, I feel his right arm seal around my neck in a chokehold.

Any other day, if my dad was to put me in a chokehold, I'd just tap out when I'd had enough. We wrestled each other even when I was in college. It was important for him to feel like he could still best me, that I was still his son. And though I'd never tell him, I let him win. It seemed so important to him, and it wasn't to me.

But this is different, because something has broken (other than my face) between my dad and I. Something has broken within him, and it feels like he's going for the kill. The choice for him is between the life of his beloved chip program and the life of his son. In his calculus, the chip program saves more lives. Keeps America safer. I'm now a threat to America's position in the world. I'm a threat to national security, even though all I'm advocating for is shutting down the chip program, not revealing our terrible secret. I guess my dad loved me enough to try to get me to change my mind, but now I'm just in the way.

A chokehold can kill a man. It can snap the windpipe or deprive the lungs and brain of oxygen for long enough. It doesn't take brawn, just technique and persistence, so it's a lethal weapon even in the hands of an elderly 150-pound man with scrawny arms. When the agents enter the room six minutes from now, my father will claim I attacked him first. Or he'll call them in. When the president arrives for an explanation, Dad will put on his second Oscar-worthy performance of the day, mourn the death of his son, and then "turn off" the chip program.

It's a good thing I'm a pessimist.

When I bandaged myself up back in the hospital, I hid a 2½-inch 18-gauge needle in the thick ACE bandage on my wrist and hand. It's not much, but it'll be enough if I can extract it quickly.

I'd initially been trying to pry my dad's forearm off my neck, but once someone has a good chokehold, that won't work. I churn my powerful legs backwards, slamming him into the wall. His grip barely loosens but he's hurt, and it gives me time to fumble with the bandage. My right thumb and forefinger finally locate the needle hub.

The room around me is beginning to dim. The feeling is reminiscent of drowning. No air in or out. I feel my mind beginning to panic, and I know I only have seconds left. This is a tiny needle, and I'm only going to get one shot. Stabbing his thigh or torso will likely have little effect on his grip around my neck.

I'm standing at the bottom of a pool, but this time I'm a grown man. I can see the surface of the water as the light pours through. I'm reaching up to it but my lower torso seems cemented to the floor. A solitary figure I can barely make out stands at the edge of the pool, looking down at me, arms folded across his chest.

Dad.

I let my hands fall to my sides, resigned to my fate.

I close my eyes, and I see Amy. And my daughters. And Angela. And Carrie. And Kwasi.

And with the needle wedged tightly between my middle and ring fingers, I thrust my right hand up as hard as I can, as if I'm giving myself a right uppercut.

The needle slices through the sinewy fibers of my dad's bicep, the tip popping out centimeters from my face. He roars in anguish and his arm drops from my neck. I rip the needle out and spin to my left, pinning my left forearm against his neck and raising my right hand to strike.

I stop inches from his terrified eye. He's still my dad. The grandfather to my kids. Even he deserves forgiveness. I loosen the pressure against his neck and lower my arm. My dad crumples to the floor, holding his arm as blood seeps through his fingers. I know I've torn some muscle tissue, ripped through some nerves and blood vessels, but I expect him to make a full recovery. I leave him slumped against the wall and go to the computer. I have work to do.

Chapter 62

2100

The agents are shocked when they find my dad bleeding on the floor. I tell them to call for medical as I put the finishing keystrokes into the system.

It's finally over.

Tomorrow will be a different day for all of us. We'll try to return to life as usual, but the scars from today will linger. And that's mostly a good thing. I am eager to get home, wash up, and see my family. An agent drives me home, and I'm pleased to find that I've beaten Amy there. She probably got caught in I-64 traffic in Yorktown.

I go upstairs to the bedroom and straight to the bathroom. I look at myself. Battered, bruised, but not destroyed. Sixteen hours ago, I woke up with the mind of an eighteen-year-old teenager, but now I'm back to myself. I know exactly who I am, the person I want to be.

I step into the shower and let the warm water wash over me for God knows how long. It feels amazing. I know it can't wash away the stain of my actions. But on the inside, I do feel a warmth, something I can't explain. On the surface it feels like gratitude. I'm alive, my family is safe, and this saga is over. But underneath, I sense something deeper. So I reach down and find out what it is.

I'm surprised by what I find. It's a peace. A belief that free will matters. That our memories are often the offspring of our choices, good and bad. Without our memories, we can't learn from the past. Our declarative memory—the material available to our conscious mind that we can store and retrieve to make decisions with—is vital. Procedural memory? Untouched by the chip. I could still ride a bike, drive a car, and do anything else I learned how to do through practice.

Where does belief, faith, fit into all this? It doesn't fit very well at all. Because I truly believe faith goes beyond what our brains can process. I'm reminded of my dear aunt, Comfort Asiedu, who was a deaconess at our church for many years. When I got married in medical school, she gave my wife and me one of our favorite registry items: a toaster oven. It's amazing what excites newlyweds. As the years passed, Auntie Comfort developed Alzheimer's. She was probably already developing it when I was in med school. It was depressing for my parents to watch their relative, a woman only a few years older than them, fall apart. She stopped recognizing close friends, would get lost driving around the neighborhood, and sometimes left food burning on the stove. That's when her family decided it was time for her to move to assisted living. As her condition deteriorated, I often thought about the chip research I was doing, and I cried thinking about the ways it could possibly help her, though we were still far away from doing human trials. My mom called one night in tears, saying that she felt like she didn't even know how to reach her sister anymore. My suggestion to her? Pray with her. Read her Bible passages. My simple, neuroscientific thought was *Alzheimer's can't touch her spirit.* My mom called back the next day overjoyed—she said she took my advice and Comfort perked up and was more lucid than she'd been for weeks.

She died a few months later, but I've never forgotten how my mom was able to reconnect with her sister during those final weeks. One could chalk it up to her memory being jogged by hearing the Scriptures. Or to the act of praying tapping into her procedural memory. Or maybe, just maybe, it's both of those plus something greater. Something that makes us humans more than the sum of our parts, more than organized atoms and molecules, more than just a brain that can store and retrieve information. My mom is more than just a brain. And while her struggle with Alzheimer's has been brief, it is still painful to watch. Even though there have only been a handful of times she hasn't recognized me, I've never once doubted that she loves me. Alzheimer's can't take that away. My dad struggles more than I do; no doubt Mom's journey fueled his obsession with memory control even further. Come to think of it, I'm sure he's chipped her. She's doing a lot better than I'd expect for someone who should be in a more advanced stage of illness. Imagine that, my chip being used for good.

I turn off the water and begin to dry off. I can hear commotion downstairs. They're home. I break into a wide smile and hurry to my closet to throw on the first set of clean clothes I see: black athletic shorts and a sleeveless yellow top. I stumble down the stairs and Ana is the first to greet me halfway down.

"Happy birthday, Daddy!" The other two are a few steps behind, and I allow myself to be enveloped by their love, plopping down on the steps wrapped in their joyous embraces. I try not to let them see me grimace as they aggravate my lumps and bruises. I give each one a firm kiss on the cheek (Kobi demands two, of course), and then I see Amy at the bottom of the steps.

"Happy birthday, Daddy Bear. You've had quite a day." She looks radiant, and behind her tired eyes, I see peace.

"Daddy? What happened to your ear?" asks Gabri, reaching at the bandages. She's going to be the kid that follows in my medical footsteps someday.

"An accident. I'll tell you about it later," I reply. "We may need to uh . . . rearrange some things in the freezer, sweetie," I say, winking at Amy. She nods and disappears around the corner.

We have a quiet birthday gathering a little while later. My mom shows up with a pot of my favorite stew; she knows home-cooking is the best gift she can give me. She tells me my dad had a late day at work and hasn't called home yet. I tell her not to worry about him. Our next-door neighbors drop by for a slice of cake. It feels good to be doing something normal.

At bedtime, I meticulously tuck each girl into bed, saying goodnight prayers and singing them a song. Each one has a special song that I wrote just for them when they were born. And even though this is part of our nighttime ritual, it feels extra special tonight.

I curl into bed beside Amy at 2155. Early for me. She snuggles in beside me and we don't say anything to each other. When you've been married for seventeen years and you're still in love, sometimes you don't need words. I pet her head gently and feel my eyes getting heavy.

Chapter 63

0820

My name is Benjamin Brew. I awake with a startle and look at my clock. It's 0820, and I never sleep this late.

I feel a bit disoriented as I roll out of bed and walk straight to the bathroom in my boxer briefs. After relieving myself, I flush the toilet and wash my hands and face. I take a long, hard look in the mirror. I'm not sure what I see.

I'm surprised to see the left side of my face is pretty swollen and there are some tiny cuts on my face. A bandage on my left ear is burgundy, soaked with dried blood. I reach up to remove it but think better of it and lower my hand. I brush my teeth, throw on the clothes that are lying on the counter, and step into my slippers.

I smell bacon cooking downstairs and it draws me like a magnet.

Midway down the stairs, I hear voices chattering in the kitchen. One of them stops me dead in my tracks.

It's my dad.

I bolt back up the stairs and grab my phone off the dresser where it charged all night. There are no missed calls. I quickly scan the contacts and press a button. After a few rings, the line is live with the jarring sound of rustling parts. I briefly hold the receiver a few inches away from my ear.

"Hello?" a muffled voice responds. "You do know it's before nine o'clock on a Saturday."

I let out a sigh of relief. Carrie.

"Are you ok, Carrie? Just wanted to check in with you." I'm trying not to sound frantic. All the travails of yesterday could have been for nothing.

"What are you talking about? Yeah, I'm fine. Just a little groggy right now." She yawns loudly. More rustling noise.

"Do you remember what happened yesterday?"

Long pause. Almost too long. "Ummm . . . sort of. Went to class . . . then it's all kinda fuzzy after that."

Sweet staff of Aaron! I failed. My mainframe codes must have not worked . . . the MRI must have failed . . . but how? How could I have been so st—

"Ha! Just messin' with you, Doc." She indulges herself with a full five seconds of laughter. "I remember everything. And the fact that I do means that you did something right. I had dinner with my dad last night and we hashed a lot of stuff out. It was great."

I want to reach through my phone and strangle her. But instead I take two deep breaths and loosen my grip on the phone. "GI—, glad you're ok. Don't forget to take your meds. Doctor's orders."

"Don't worry," she says. "That was never *my* problem."

I hang up and slide the phone into my pocket. This time, I walk down the stairs with a little more confidence. My dad and Amy are sitting on the kitchen bar stools. Ana, my little master chef in the making, is flipping the bacon. Gabs and Kobi must be sleeping in.

"Morning, Ames. Morning, Dad. 'Sup, Ana."

Their heads swivel in unison to greet me.

"Happy birthday, son!" my dad exclaims, though underneath I hear strain and weakness in his voice. "I seem to have had quite the day yesterday. Apparently I fell down a flight of stairs at work and hurt my arm. I don't remember much. Scared your mother to death— she ran back to the car to get my pain medicine." He pauses to gingerly rub the portion of his arm not wrapped in a half-inch layer of gauze. "Maybe it's this damn headache. Last few days seem hazy. Haven't ever missed your birthday, though. So sorry." He gives me a once-over and adds, "Hell, you look like you fell down *three* flights of stairs."

Amy pats him on the back and chuckles. "I think we're all getting a little older. I can remember our little party last night, but not much else. Your face, Ben . . . I certainly don't remember you falling down the stairs. How much did I drink?" she asks, looking pensively into the coffee cup in her right hand.

Ana shakes her head at me disapprovingly. "Please tell me you haven't joined a fight club."

I wave my hands in front of me to ward off their concern, then give each of them a brief hug before hoisting myself onto a stool between Amy and Dad. "Yesterday was a day to forget," I say with a shrug. "Let's make this one a day to remember."

THE END

ABOUT THE AUTHOR

A graduate of Harvard College and the Yale School of Medicine, Kwabena "Bobo" Blankson is a pediatrician with subspecialty training in adolescent medicine. He has more than thirteen years of military experience. Dr. Bobo has published in peer-reviewed journals on adolescent healthcare utilization, obesity, and energy-drink consumption, and has been featured on Oprah.com, NYTimes.com, HuffingtonPost.com, CNN.com, Time.com, Forbes.com, CBSnews.com and more. He is passionate about teen and young adult health, and in 2015 he joined Girls to Women Health and Wellness, a medical practice in Dallas, to help launch Young Men's Health and Wellness. His hobbies include sports, music, video gaming, reading, and cooking. He is the author of *The Saucier's Bones*, a middle-grade, recipe-filled adventure novel. Dr. Bobo lives in Dallas with his wife and three daughters.

Made in the USA
Coppell, TX
11 May 2021